# COUSIN IN LOVE

## THE END OF THE PROLETARIAT RISING

Charles Jackson

Author's Tranquility Press
Marietta, Georgia

Charles Jackson/Author's Tranquility Press
2706 Station Club Drive SW
Marietta, GA 30060
www.authorstranquilitypress.com

Publisher's Note: This is a work of fiction. Names, characters, places, and incidents are a product of the author's imagination. Locales and public names are sometimes used for atmospheric purposes. Any resemblance to actual people, living or dead, or to businesses, companies, events, institutions, or locales is completely coincidental.

Ordering Information:
Quantity sales. Special discounts are available on quantity purchases by corporations, associations, and others. For details, contact the "Special Sales Department" at the address above.

COUSIN IN LOVE/ Charles Jackson
Paperback: 978-1-958554-44-9
eBook: 978-1-958554-45-6

# *Table of Contents*

INTRODUCTION

# THE STORY OF COUSIN IN LOVE

To the readers, this is a story about a boy name Anthony. Anthony was about five foot and six inches tall, showing brown eyes with black curly hair. He was born in San Antonio, TX from a father who was in the Air Force but raised in Winston Salem, NC. His father's name was Richland Jackson. Anthony's mother was an ambitious woman born in Winston Salem, N.C. His mother's name was Dee Jackson. Anthony lived a brief period in San Antonio with his parents and brother. His parents were not rich because they continued to be ambitious. Anthony's father retired from cleaning planes at an aviation company. By the time Anthony parents retired, they became divorced from each other. Later, in life, Anthony learned he obtained his ambitions from his parents. In return, Anthony's parents got their ambitions from their parents.

Dee Jackson's father and mother were married at a young age. They raised five children including my mother and lived prosperous lives. Anthony's grandparents, who were Dee Jackson's parents, owned a laundry mat and a convenience store. In addition, the children managed their own careers, as they got older. Anthony had an aunt who own her own sewing business. Including an aunt, who preached in her own church and an aunt, who worked at a brewery factory. Uncle Kay Harris, who was the only son, moved to New Jersey to sell food produce. Then, the youngest child my mother, who worked as a supervisor at a distribution company.

Nevertheless, to be honest, Anthony and his brother lived a modest life in the 1970's. From the first day, Anthony remembers his parents lecturing to be all you can be. Anthony's parents always made circumstances proving if you do your best that love would come pouring out. For example, Anthony's brother B.J and Anthony would be playing in the living room. Richland Jackson would request anyone of his children to bring him a drink. The first time, Anthony made a drink for his dad, it was a whiskey sour.

Richland Jackson replied, "Son bring me a whiskey sour."

Anthony replied, "How do you make that?"

Richland Jackson replied, "Well it is easy. I will tell you step by step how to do it, when you reach the bar."

Anthony replied, "Okay, I am at the bar."

Richland Jackson replied, "When you see an aluminum vase with a funny shape top, open the top and add ice, until it is halfway full. Then, fill the vase with whiskey about a third ways and pour the sour mix until it rises halfway. I call the vase a shaker. Shake the shaker a couple of times until it gets cold and then pour the drink in a glass."

Anthony completed the task as his father was instructing him. He gave the drink to his father Richland Jackson. Richland Jackson tasted the drink and gave Anthony a thumbs up signaling to show how good the drink was to him.

Richland Jackson replied, "If you can make drinks this good, you can hang with me all night."

Anthony replied, "Mom can I make you a drink also."

Dee Jackson replied, "No, I do not think so. If you would just give me a beer."

Anthony's brother B.J, he was already indoctrinated in the techniques of bartending, compliments of the Jackson family. B.J was mixing and serving drinks, before Anthony started walking. He was four years older than his brother was and assisted Richland Jackson with the family training. If Anthony's parents were not watching him, B.J believed it was his duty to keep his brother in check.

B.J replied, "Hey little brother, if you stay out of trouble and put a smile on our parents face, the world is ours."

This philosophy was true in most cases, not just for making drinks. It was the case for doing well in school, doing the housework, and dating girls. Richland Jackson attitude was a little different from the mother's position. However, one thing they both agreed upon was when they children find a mate, the girl had to be compatible with the child. The girl personality had to be strong for the boy to be strong. In addition, the girl must let the boy become what a boy is going to become.

B.J philosophy was very different. His wish was the girl had to be rich. B.J wanted the girl to have enough money where, if he did not want to spend money, she would have enough for two. B.J did not care if the girl was smart or dumb. Education was a plus and compatibility was superstition. Love was a word made up to influence someone into thinking, they were more important than the majority. The only thing B.J really understood was money and more money.

Anthony took a different look at life. He believed; if you work very hard, it did not matter what the other person has. Everything will fall in place with compatibility or money, if you work hard at it. Anthony prayed; he would not have to search for the right girl. His prediction was God would hand carry the most attractive girl, he had ever seen right to him. Fast-talking would not be required because the girl would say exactly, what's on her mind to start a love connection between the two of them.

Later, in life, the differences of B.J and Anthony chose them to separate. They lived completely different lives. At one point in their lives when there where disagreements, B.J and Anthony only encounter was brief discussions, when met between the two. This was done during the morning before school and at nighttime when going to bed. Their parents kept close watch of their sons. Their parents began to discuss in private, what directions their sons where taking.

When Richland Jackson retired from the Air Force, he relocated his family to Winston Salem, NC by the request of Dee Jackson. This was the location where the parents were raised, met and became married. Richland Jackson purchased a house on the south side of town. Anthony remembered this home, as their first permanent place of residence. It was a nice starter home. During the 1970's, integration was still fresh. Anthony's parents were the first black family in the neighborhood. Anthony's brother B.J advised Anthony not to wonder alone in the street. Anthony reached 8 years old at this time and his brother was 12 years old. Their mother Dee Jackson, she would drive them to school before she would go to work. Dee Jackson obtained a job for a company and was making good money. The daddy Richland Jackson, he received a good job working at a cigarette company. The family was doing well financially.

Then, a neighbor next door introduced himself to the family. The neighbor who was white, had children who were close to B.J and Anthony age. The children consisted of a boy name Gregg and his little sister's name Judy. They were a strange pair of siblings because Gregg would have Judy to do strange things. For example, B.J and Anthony would be playing in their backyard, when Gregg and Judy would visit with their dog.

Gregg replied, "Hi neighbor, what are you doing?"

B.J replied, "Nothing."

Gregg replied, "B.J let us go somewhere private, as around the front house and talk because we are older. My sister and your little brother do not need to hear our words."

B.J replied, "This is fine but wait one second. Your dog is dropping waste in our yard."

Gregg replied, "Judy, I have told you about bringing the dog."

Judy replied, "I had to take him so; he would not run away."

Gregg replied, "Okay but; the dog is dropping waste in the neighbor yard. Judy, I want you to pick up the dog waste with your hands and throw it away."

B.J replied, "Gregg wouldn't Judy need a newspaper or something to pick up the dog waste?"

Gregg replied, "No need; Judy will do anything, I tell her to do. She is stupid".

Judy politely apologized to B.J and Anthony. She carried the dog waste bare hand in one hand and the dog with the other. Judy walked across the street and departed to her home. B.J glared at Anthony in a peculiar way and follow Gregg around the side of the house. Anthony could tell B.J had a problem with what he heard and witnessed at Gregg actions towards his sister.

B.J replied, "Gregg our neighbor across the street is crazy. He insisted, Judy is a whore. Gregg notified him; if he wanted to have sex, just let him know because he will get his sister to do it free".

Anthony replied, "This is too crazy; Gregg makes Judy do sex acts. What kind of brother is this? Why is he so mean to Judy?"

B.J replied, "I do not believe, Gregg cares much about anything. Gregg has a problem in my eyes."

On another day, Anthony was playing in his front yard on his steps alone. He heard a voice singing outside across the street. Anthony raised his head up to look across the street to see, who was singing. It was Judy singing in her front yard. Judy waved at him; he waved back. Anthony started thinking about what Gregg said about his sister and how wrong Gregg treated his sister. He stood up and seen Judy coming across the street towards him.

Judy replied, "Hey Anthony; want to play with me?"

Anthony replied, "Sure, what are you doing?"

Judy replied, "I am playing tea. Anthony, do you want some tea?"

Anthony replied, "Sure, I will take some, if you are going to give me some".

Judy replied, "I have some at my house. How about we go to my bedroom, where I have a tea table and tea set already displayed."

Anthony replied, "Okay, not thinking he would get in trouble".

When Anthony arrived with Judy to her house, Judy opened the door; and they greeted her dog Benji. Then, her mother came out the kitchen; and Judy introduced Anthony to her mother. Judy told her mother this is Anthony; and we are going to play tea in my bedroom.

Judy's mother replied, "It is fine, just let the bedroom door stay open".

Judy and Anthony played tea for about an hour, pretending to drink tea from her tea set.

Anthony replied, "Judy this is very nice of you to invite me to your home".

Judy replied, "You are welcome; besides I do not have any friends anyway to play with."

Anthony replied, "I do not have any friends either".

Judy replied, "Well that is good. How about you become my friend?

Anthony was about to say something but, Gregg entered the house. Gregg just looked at Anthony.

Gregg replied, "What are you doing here Anthony?

Anthony replied, "I am just playing with your sister".

Gregg replied, "Who gave you permission, you can play with my sister?"

Anthony replied, "Your mother did".

Gregg replied, "I am just joking with you. Anthony, you like my sister?"

Anthony replied, "Yes, she is pretty cool".

Gregg replied, "Anthony would you like to make out with her?"

Anthony hesitated speaking and watched Judy play.

Anthony replied, "Gregg, I am only eight years old".

Gregg replied, "I can make her do freaky things to you, ask your brother".

Anthony replied, "No thanks Gregg, I do not want to take advantage of your sister. I like your sister as a friend".

Gregg replied, "It is a shame, Anthony. I want to tell you; Judy is a whore! Nobody should be friends with a whore".

Anthony replied, "Gregg something is definitely wrong with you".

Gregg replied, "Anthony sees the whore done got you in trouble! Your family is looking for you Anthony".

Anthony begins to remember, what his brother told him. B.J told him not to go anywhere unless somebody is with him in the family. Anthony jumps up to inform Judy goodbye. During the same time, Judy stands up and gives him a kiss on the cheek.

Judy replied, "I will see you tomorrow Anthony".

After Anthony arrived at his home, his parents scolded him very bad. They reinstated no visiting other neighbors without permission. Anthony explained, where he was located; and his brother overheard the conversation. B.J scolded Anthony, after reminding him no wondering house to house, unless he was with him.

Anthony acknowledged to B.J; he enjoyed playing with Judy. Judy does not have any friends. She is nice but; her brother is abusive to her.

B.J replied, "Anthony, I do not want you to interfere with the neighbor's problems. The stuff Gregg and Judy do are they concerns".

Anthony replied, "I like Judy. If I see her brother mistreating her, for now own I am going to say something to him".

B.J replied, "Anthony, if you get involved, it is on your behalf. I am going to keep my mouth closed".

The next day after school, Anthony observed his brother given Gregg some money. B.J, Gregg, and Judy walked around an abandon home up the street. First, Judy comes from the house smiling, while wiping her face. Next, B.J travels behind her smiling, while buttoning up his pants; and Gregg is expressing his point of view. Anthony studies they position and strutted in their directions. B.J notices Anthony and gives him a mean look.

B.J replied, "I think you are becoming like Judy, stupid. How many times, I must tell you; wondering from house to house is no good?"

Anthony replied, "How come I have to stay home? You leave the house".

B.J replied, "Judy and you are made for each other. I am older and wiser. When you become twelve like me then, you can walk to another house alone. Mother has already told you. The next time, it is going to be bad for you".

Anthony departed the scene and returned home. When he arrived, Judy was waiting at his doorstep with Benjie in her hand.

Judy replied, "Hello Anthony, "how are you doing?"

Anthony replied, "Judy, I am mad; do not talk to me. I think you will do anything; your brother tells you to do".

Judy replied, "Anthony, I think we need to talk in private".

Judy and Anthony walked around the back of Anthony home. They hide behind some bushes. Judy stares in Anthony eyes with a worried look. Judy gives Anthony a big hug.

Judy replied, "I do not want to do this. I wanted to wait for the right time".

Anthony replied, "What right time?"

Judy replied, "Anthony come close to me".

Anthony gets really close to Judy. Judy whispers in his ear; "Do not be afraid. I am not about to hurt you". Judy begins to kiss him on the cheek and tries to put her hand down his pants. Anthony becomes excited and backs away. He begins to feel disrespected.

Judy replied, "Anthony, why you back away? I know, I was not hurting you".

Anthony replied, "No, I am fine. What in the world, was you trying to do?"

Judy replied, "I am trying to be your girlfriend dude".

Next, Judy hears Gregg calling her.

Gregg replied, "Judy where are you located?"

Judy replied, "I am coming Gregg. Anthony, we need to finish this situation another time".

Anthony replied, "Go see your brother Judy".

Judy walked away in Gregg direction. Anthony followed behind. When they reached Gregg, he was holding Benji the dog. B.J was standing beside Gregg, as if he was waiting for something to happen.

Gregg replied, "Benji has let out some dog waste in our neighbor yard again. Where were you and why is Benji roaming in the neighbor's yard? I am going to have to discipline you about this dog. Judy, I want you to pick the dog waste up and eat it".

Judy replied, "Gregg come on; do I have to!"

Gregg replied, "Yes".

## CHAPTER TWO

# TRIP TO NY

Judy grabbed the waste out the yard with her hand and closed her eyes, as she consumed the dog waste. Anthony and his brother could not believe, what they had seen. B.J became upset.

B.J replied, "Gregg, this is the last straw. We are no longer friends anymore. I cannot stand here and allow you to treat your sister as this anymore. You are treating her as an animal. Please leave and take your sister with you. I do not ever want to see you or your sister over here again".

Judy replied, "Well, I still can continue and visit Anthony sometimes".

Anthony replied, "No Judy, my standards are too high to deal with this also".

After the incident, B.J and Anthony never interacted with the neighbors again. They heard rumors of Gregg's father was abusive to Gregg and his entire family. In return, this caused Gregg to become abusive to Judy. During the end of the year, police placed Gregg's father in jail for selling drugs and Gregg's parents became divorced. A Psychologist for mental problems, treated Gregg and Judy both. In the end, both Gregg and Judy learned better behaviors with each other through training. In the end, Anthony forgot about his neighbors and concentrated on meeting new people.

One day, Anthony's father announced; it was time for the family to take a trip. Anthony's father dreamed of the family going to New York and to visit Uncle West and Aunt East. Anthony's father and mother began having relationship problems because of stress. The parents worked very hard and seldom took time away from their jobs. Richland Jackson figured a trip would relieve some of the stress of working, the stress of children finding someone to socialize with them and the stress of prejudice in the neighborhood. When Richland Jackson notified the family of his decision, everyone was happy.

Dee Jackson replied, "Finally the family is getting away. The children first trip from North Carolina, since leaving Texas".

B.J replied, "I cannot wait. Finally, I get to meet some city girls".

Anthony replied, "I just want to spend time with my cousins and get away".

Richland Jackson owned a station wagon so; when school season ended, everyone piled in the automobile and prepared to ride to New York for the summer. Along during the ride, B.J informed Anthony, not to try to get in his way by hanging around him.

B.J replied, "I already know those New York girls are going to try to talk to me".

Anthony replied, "I am not even thinking about those girls. I am really thinking about spending my time with my cousins. B.J, how you going to think about a girl in New York, when mom says you have too many girlfriends at home?"

B.J replied, "There is no way, I am going to go the whole summer in New York without finding some fine New York girls to be my sugar-baby for the summer".

When the family and Anthony arrived at their destination in New York, Anthony was ten now. Where Anthony's relatives lived in New York, it was a beautiful place. The first reaction entering the house, Anthony headed to his cousins and gave each of them a handshake. Then, Anthony located his aunt and uncle, while giving them a big hug. A feeling of excitement traveled from the top to the bottom of his body. Anthony was so happy; he could not control his emotions. He realized finally; he was in a place, where his family was at peace. Everybody was talking and greeting each other with joy. The feeling was similar, as waiting for Christmas; and it finally came.

Then, a surprise event occurred. Aunt East announced, there was an unknown visitor in her house. Someone who Anthony has never met before. Aunt East introduced the family to her newest member. This person was a Puerto Rican girl, who was slender built with short hair and walked with a finesse. The girl nickname was Kat.

Kat replied, "How are you doing everyone. It was so good to see family from North Carolina because I have relatives who resides in Winston Salem, NC. I know nothing about North Carolina".

B.J replied, "Great! It is the city, we live in. Maybe one day Kat, you can come down and visit".

Kat replied, "I would like this".

The story on Kat was Aunt East had met Kat through her mother who became good friends of Aunt East. Aunt East and Kat mother were very good friends. Although, Kat mother had an alcohol-drinking problem and had to give up rights to Kat because of unknown events. Aunt East in Kat's defense, volunteered to keep Kat until Kat's mother detox in an Alcohol rehab place in Winston Salem, NC and became equipped to establish her rights as custody of Kat again. The only drawback was Kat found ways to get into trouble by acting older than her age and by disrespecting authority.

Uncle West was training Anthony how to paint, when Kat started to take interest of Anthony. On one occasion, Anthony was painting in the basement.

Kat replied, "Anthony is your name right. How are you doing? I just want to know, what relationship you are to Ms. East?"

Anthony replied, "Ms. East and Mr. West are my aunt and uncle".

Kat replied, "Right, this is nice. My mother is a friend of Ms. East. Ms. East visited my mother; and they locked her up in jail. My mother is a child abuser. Ms. East saved me from my mother".

Kat replied, "My father left home and never returned. I believe, I will be residing here for a couple of days".

Anthony replied, "I am sorry for your situation".

Kat replied, "How long are you going to be staying here?"

Anthony replied, "I will be here probable, the entire summer. My brother B.J and I are going to be here until school starts back in my hometown".

Kat replied smiling, "I think, I am going to like this. Since Anthony, you are going to be here; I am going to ask Aunt East, can I stay for the summer too. Anthony is it okay with you?" Kat looks at him up and down".

Anthony replied, "Kat, it is fine with me".

Kat replied, "So Anthony, do you have a girlfriend in North Carolina?"

Anthony replied, "No, I am not dating. I do not believe; my mother would approve of me dating at a young age".

Kat replied, "I think every boy should have a girlfriend. Anthony, it is not good to be alone. I heard a person can go crazy, if he does not have a friend. Anthony, if you want me too; I will be your girlfriend, while we are here this summer".

Anthony was astonished by the remarks Kat made. Kat was a pretty Puerto Rican girl. Anthony could not believe, Kat actions and comments. He figured Kat had to be playing a trick because no girl ever acted like this towards him. B.J overheard the conversation without Anthony knowledge. B.J talked to Anthony at bedtime about the conversation between Kat and Anthony.

B.J replied, "Kat wants you Anthony, I can tell. Anthony, I need to inform you; Puerto Rican girls are sex crazy. I am going to have to teach you some things because you are inexperience with girls".

Anthony replied, "Why you need to teach me? I am not worried about Kat. I am good because we are just friends. Kat is not going to have sex with me or anybody else. I believe she is playing a trick on me".

B.J replied, "Anthony wakes up, this is not a trick. Kat is not playing no games. Anthony, you need to be prepared because Kat is going to ask you for sex. My question is do you like Kat? If you do then, this will be your first experience with sex. Kat appears to be experience too; just do whatever she tells you to do. If Kat do ask you about sex, then, just say yes to everything. Anthony, I know you are only ten but; sex will help you mature".

After his brother spoke, Anthony refused to seriously take B.J advice. The next day, Uncle West requested for Anthony to come down to the basement.

Uncle West replied, "Anthony, I need you to come down to the basement. I can teach you how to interior paint, while we listen to some great vintage music".

Anthony replied, "Sure Uncle West, I am on the way".

Kat replied, "Anthony are you going down to the basement".

Anthony replied, "Yes".

Kat replied, "I will meet you down there".

Anthony was confused by Kat's comments. He walked down the stairs to the basement. When Anthony arrived in the basement, he noticed; Kat wearing her night gown and sitting on the sofa, while watching T.V. Anthony heard his Uncle West in another room with vintage music playing. His Uncle West was shouting, "Anthony do not be shy, come on in hear because I have some panting tips". Anthony walked by Kat on the sofa; and she winks her eye at him. Kat raises her night gown up and shows her underwear. Anthony was in disbelief. He notified B.J later, what happen during the night.

B.J replied, "Anthony, I told you. Kat, she wants you. It is just a matter of time, before she throws herself at you".

Anthony replied, "B.J, I think you are right".

B.J replied, "I know, I am right. I am going to tell you, what you should do. I want you, Anthony to meet Kat in the basement. I will be there to assist, what to say to Kat, when the moment happens".

Anthony replied, "Okay, I will set it up. I will tell her to meet me in the basement in the morning".

The next morning, Anthony meets Kat in the basement, while Anthony's brother sits on the basement steps.

Kat replied, "Hey baby, while I have my fancy pajamas on, come sit beside me on the sofa".

Anthony replied nervously, "Alright".

B.J replied whispering, "Go ahead Anthony, sit beside her".

Anthony sits beside Kat; and she begins kissing him. Then, Kat stretched him out on the couch, the long way. Kat laid on top of Anthony and rolled him on top of her. B.J decided to come downstairs so; he can maneuver Anthony's body. He pushes Anthony's bottom up and down, while Anthony was on top of Kat. Anthony jumped up and screamed stop...stop...stop! Kat jumped up and observed; B.J running in the next room. Kat begins to laugh. Anthony figured; after all this, his chances were lost with Kat now.

In the end, Kat laughed and joked about the whole situation. During the rest of the summer, Kat and Anthony continued being close. They became close friends. Anthony and his family returned to North Carolina to prepare for school season. Aunt East filed for adoption on Kat to receive tax benefits. Kat ran away from Aunt East to be with her mother in North Carolina. Kat contacted Anthony, when she settled with her relatives in North Carolina. Then, Anthony began to date Kat once again.

One day, Kat and Anthony decided to attend a Prince concert together, close to their area. It was their first time going to a concert together. Anthony arranged for his aunt to drive them to the concert. Once they arrived, Anthony noticed; a change in Kat personality. Kat turned quiet and secretive. Prince announced during his concert, he was given a backstage after party show. Anthony notified; Kat ahead of time, they had a curfew. The rule was to meet Anthony's Aunt after the concert. Kat had different plans. She disappeared, when the concert ended. Anthony never heard anything else from Kat again. The next day, Anthony tried to get in contact with Kat but; she never returned his phone calls. This was the last time, he met with Kat. Anthony just assumed; Kat was not interested in having a relationship with him; or she did not care anymore.

B.J was always concerned about Anthony. He would tell Anthony, you are going to be old and gray, before you find the right girlfriend. Another saying of his was you would have better luck finding an ugly girlfriend because she would be glad to have you. Also, B.J replied, "When I was your age, I was making love to all the girls in my school". In addition, Anthony's mother would advise him too on girls. Dee Jackson told him to pick the girls to date, who parents have money. This way Anthony, you would not have to worry, if she likes you are not because she will not use you for your own money.

Eventually, Anthony's family moved from the south side of Winston Salem to the north side of town. The relocation effected Anthony's social relationship status. At the old residence, Anthony had started to build a friendship base. When the movement was completed, Anthony social status became non-existing. Anthony had no friends or family in this new neighborhood. He became sad and secluded. Anthony's family was the only Black family in the neighborhood once again.

Then, one day, another black family move into their neighborhood. The Black family lived right across the street from Anthony's location. B.J notified Anthony; he observed a girl around about Anthony's age. Anthony had just turned twelve. The family across the street was unpacking their van. B.J instructed Anthony; go to the mailbox and pretend to check for mail. Then, when a girl returns to unload her family's van, politely say hello and tell her your name.

Anthony walked outside the mailboxes. When he arrived there, a girl name Alisa was standing by the mailboxes. Alisa was approximately two inches shorter than himself, slender built and sarcastic with her language. Before Anthony could speak a word, Alisa inquired how old are you?

Anthony replied, "My name is Anthony; and I am twelve years old".

Alisa replied, "Did I ask you, your name? Besides, you don't appear to be twelve years old to me".

Anthony replied, "No and yes, I am twelve".

Alisa replied, "You trying to play games with me. What is it, no or yes?"

Anthony replied, "Yes".

Alisa replied, "If you are twelve, what month was you born?"

Anthony replied, "The month of May".

Alisa replied, "I am still older because I was born in Jan. What grade are you in?"

Anthony replied, "I am in the seventh grade and going to Mineral Springs, which is the school behind our house".

Alisa replied, "This is perfect because we will be going to school together". Alright neighbor, please allow me to introduce you to myself. I am Alisa. I live with my parents and have two brothers".

Alisa's parents were very nice. They treated Anthony, as if he was their own son. Alisa's brothers were very supportive as well. When anytime there was a problem in the neighborhood, they tried to help. They informed Anthony exactly, what was happening in their community. The younger brother even attempted to train Anthony on the fundamentals of sports. Anthony was very pleased with his neighbors. Although, he believed Alisa had something to prove from the start of their introduction.

One day, Alisa's younger brother was training Anthony how to play basketball. Alisa's younger brother informed Anthony; he is two years older so, Anthony should be playing with someone else his own age.

He also replied, "Anthony, you might be a good guy but; how come you do not spend any time with someone else your own age?"

It really hurt Anthony feelings because he knew no one else to play with in his neighborhood. The next day, Anthony was playing basketball alone in his parents' driveway and Alisa appeared.

Alisa replied, "Can I borrow the basketball for a second. I would like to show you something".

Anthony replied, "Sure".

Anthony tossed the ball to Alisa. Alisa counted steps from his homemade basketball goal to an estimated distance, which resembled a free throw line. She aimed and threw the ball straight in the hoop. Anthony could not believe his eyes. In addition, Alisa could also dribble good, just as she could shoot good.

Anthony replied, "Where did you learn how to play basketball this good?"

Alisa replied, "My brothers taught me. When basketball season starts, I am trying out for the girls' basketball team in school.

From then, every time Anthony would be playing basketball outside on the side of his house, Alisa would appear. Alisa and Anthony would play free throw shooting contest, make up shoots contest and one on one contest. During the one-on-one contest, a few games Alisa would win but; mostly Anthony would find some way to cheat and cause the game to error. One game played; Alisa was defending Anthony from the basket goal real hard. Alisa tried to block Anthony's path by bumping Anthony with her body. The physical contact Alisa was doing, caused Anthony to stop playing basketball.

Alisa replied, "What is the matter? Why you stopped playing?"

Anthony replied, "Alisa, you are getting a little too physical".

Alisa replied, "What, you do not like a little physical contact from a girl?"

CHAPTERTHREE

# THIRTEENTH BIRTHDAY

Anthony replied, "No, this is not the problem. I do not care about being physical with a girl. A matter of fact, I like girls".

Alisa replied, "Okay then, I am a girl. What is wrong with me?"

Anthony replied, "Nothing is wrong with you except, you are my friend".

After Anthony informed Alisa of this, Alisa treated Anthony differently. Alisa stopped playing basketball with Anthony. Later during the week, Anthony overheard Alisa's brother saying to Alisa, "No guy is interested in a girl who can beat him in basketball". Anthony noticed; this made Alisa sad. Anthony felt sort of bad; he did not realize, Alisa playing basketball would cause their relationship to change. He had placed Alisa in the friendship zone without realizing it. Alisa was cute but; she was a Tomboy. Anthony never encountered a girl who was tough as him. Alisa's brother became disappointed because Alisa and Anthony were not playing together anymore. The only conclusion, Anthony could understand was maybe, Alisa's brother wanted something more to happen between

Alisa and him. Maybe, Alisa's brother wanted Alisa and him to date.

Anthony found out; his brother was upset. B.J notified his mom Dee Jackson.

B.J replied, "Hey mom, I cannot believe, Anthony has not asked the cute girl across the street out yet. I am wondering, what is the problem. It appears to me; he just passes by on all the nice girls. Anthony treats her, as if she is one of the guys. I am starting to believe; he does not know, how to pick a girlfriend".

One day, Alisa visited Anthony. Anthony introduced Alisa to his mother for the first time.

Dee Jackson replied, "Nice to meet you, Alisa. Greetings, you are our newest neighbor. I have heard so much about you. I would like to know one thing. When you and my son are going to start dating?"

Anthony replied, "Mom, Alisa and I are just friends! This is not a fair question at all to be asking".

Dee Jackson replied, "I just want the both of you to know; if you are dating, you have my approval".

Anthony replied, "I figured this much but; Alisa is only interested in basketball. Alisa is trying out for the girls' basketball team. She is not trying to date anyone".

After Alisa overheard Anthony make this comment, she glanced at Anthony with a disapproval look. Dee Jackson shook her head with disbelief. After Alisa left, she informed Anthony; he has a lot to learn about what to say around girls his age.

Dee Jackson replied, "Anthony, let me tell you something right now. You are young and will be turning thirteen on your next birthday. I am going to give you a birthday party. What you can do is create a guest list of people to invite. Invite all your friends, which you know in the neighborhood".

Anthony replied, "Right now, the only friend in the neighborhood I have is Alisa".

Dee Jackson replied, "Alright then Anthony, you can invite some of your friends from school. I know you probably have friends in school".

Anthony replied, "I do but; I am sure they will have transportation problems. How about I invite a few of my cousins over, including Alisa, and her brothers".

Dee Jackson replied, "This is fine with me. It is going to be your birthday party".

Anthony phone calls a few of his cousins to invite them to his birthday party. He notified Alisa on the phone of his birthday party. Alisa alerts Anthony, she will come but; she is bringing a friend. She confirms; she has a friend name Julie, who has a crush on him. Alisa requested; Anthony to invite Julie to his party because it appeared, he was not interested in her.

Alisa replied, "I hook you up with a date; and in return, you hook me up with a date".

Anthony replied, "No problem".

Anthony knew he did not have a problem fixing Alisa with a date because she was attractive but; on the other side, she was boyish. In conclusion, it was a turn off for him but; a lot of guys did not mind. Anthony invited his classmate Ricky to be Alisa date because they communicated a lot in school. Ricky had met Alisa in school so; he did not mind going on a date with Alisa.

Anthony thought; at first, no way. Julie was overweight, had gap teeth, and disgruntle. Julie also was two years and two grades in school below Anthony. Anthony figured; the only thing Julie and he had in common was they would talk about his accomplishments.

Julie enjoyed everything about Anthony. Julie was happier talking to Anthony than her own family. She dreamed only about spending time with Anthony. When Alisa and Julie communicated, the conversation always ended with Julie inquiring have you heard anything about Anthony. Other guys which greeted Julie, usually would get the cold shoulder. Julie however treated Anthony differently because she thought; he was nice. Alisa figured; if Julie liked Anthony this much, she could use this to her advantage.

Anthony realized although; he wanted people to come to his party not because he like them but, to make his party interesting. Who cares if he thought the person was unattractive because the only thing which mattered were, they were not crazy? Besides, Anthony was told in his life, one man's trash is another man's treasure. To make it short, Anthony wanted real people who were different than the average person at his party. Anthony did not have a lot of friends but; one thing he did have was interesting people on his guest list. Also, the people who he invited, he trusted they would attend because they loved a good party.

When Anthony had his birthday party, everyone on his guest list attended. Alisa was there, classmate Ricky arrived, and for sure Julie was present. Also, all his wonderful family members, including his cousins was there. The birthday party started perfectly and then; it became weird. It all happened, when Anthony's mother Dee Jackson requested Anthony to blow out the candles on his cake and make a wish. Anthony's brother B.J stood up in front of everybody with his comment.

B.J replied, "Happy birthday to my brother; and I hope he gets lucky with a girl tonight because he is driving me crazy".

Dee Jackson replied, "Happy birthday son; I am your mother; and I will tell you, not to pay attention to your brother. Besides, I have taken the liberty to talk with my best friend about you. Her name is Stacy; and she has four daughters close to your age, whom I think you will have some interest with".

Anthony's cousin Bernard taps him on the shoulder.

Bernard replied, "Anthony, you do not have to worry about all of this. I know you feel ashamed because nobody wants to be set up on a date, especially by their mom. I can introduce you to some girls and let you pick a girlfriend. I can do better than this; I can teach you how to talk with girls and get your own date. We can hang out in my neighborhood, where there is lots of pretty girls".

It became odd to Anthony, listen to everyone trying to solve his dating issues.

Alisa replied, "Wait everyone, I have found the answer to Anthony's problem. This is Anthony's new girlfriend Julie. Julie come tell everybody, Anthony and you are going to be dating".

After that statement, Anthony had heard enough of the subject. On top of everything, Anthony had another cousin who was going through a similar predicament. Anthony's cousin Ronald had dating problems too but; everyone assumed he was gay. For some reason, Ronald felted as if sharing his life to everybody.

Ronald replied, "I know the feeling, Anthony. To find someone which you can associate with is hard work".

Bernard replied, "Cousin Ronald and Cousin Anthony, I feel so sorry for them. If they did not have bad luck, they would not have luck at all. They are the same".

Anthony resented this comment. After the birthday party, Anthony had a sleepover. All the females slept in one area and the males in another area. Anthony's cousin Bernard tried to instruct his cousin Ronald on how to date a girl.

Bernard replied, "Anthony and Ronald, you all are at the right age to find the girl of your dreams. This is what you do. A pretty girl is at the drinking fountain in school. What do you do?"

Anthony replied, "Watch and observe how pretty she is".

Bernard replied, "Wrong answer, this is your opportunity to make a move. Anthony, you walk over and say, "Baby you are so fine; I just want to pat your behind. Then, you rub on her booty".

Anthony replied, "Bernard, have you lost your mind".

Bernard replied, "No! I have certainly not lost my mind. Ronald, come on and demonstrate on me. Show your cousin, how a guy supposed to do, when he spots a pretty girl bending over and drinking water out of a school water fountain".

Anthony observed Cousin Bernard bending over, as if he was drinking water out of a water fountain. Cousin Ronald walked over behind him and rubs his booty, before telling him he is so fine. Anthony watched; and it seemed as if two gay boys were being intermix, as one was rubbing the other's bottom side. The rest of the guys sleeping over, observed in a strange disbelief, while walking away.

Anthony's cousin Carl shakes his head in disgust.

Carl replied, "I told you Anthony, Ronald is gay as he wants to be. I hope you are not trying to learn anything from these guys. Anthony, just come to my house tomorrow; and I will introduce you to some girls in my neighborhood".

Anthony replied, "Okay, I will ask my mom tomorrow".

Bernard replied, "Hold up Anthony, class is closed because your cousin Ronald went overboard with the rubbing. I promise you, if you come to my house tomorrow, I will get you a girlfriend. I have plenty of girlfriends to spare".

The next day, after everything had settled, Bernard and Anthony were transported to Bernard's mother's apartment.

Bernard's mother was nice. She allowed Bernard and Anthony to sit on her front porch, where they could talk.

Bernard replied, "Today cousin, this is your day".

Anthony replied, "Why is this".

Bernard replied, "You are thirteen. I am going to show you how, I meet the girls".

There were five girls in his neighborhood standing on the corner. Bernard and Anthony walked over to the girls. Bernard requested a phone number from one of the girls. Then, he asked could we meet them later. After this, Bernard grabs my arm and pulls me away from one of the girls.

Bernard replied, "Hey Anthony, are you afraid of sex".

Anthony replied, "Bernard, I just introduce myself to these girls. I am not going to have sex with these girls".

Bernard replied, "Anthony, I understand the reason you cannot find a girlfriend. You are too scared to have sex. I am going around the corner with this girl to have a good time. I will be right back".

Anthony waited for about fifteen minutes. Bernard returned with an unhappy expression on his face at his mother's apartment.

Anthony replied, "Bernard is everything alright?"

Bernard replied, "Darn no! I don't think so. Maybe something was wrong with this girl".

Anthony replied, "Bernard did you use protection".

Bernard replied, "No, I didn't have no protection to use. I should have listened to your advice and just conversated with those girls on the corner".

Anthony replied, "I think you need to tell your mother; you need to go to the clinic".

Bernard replied, "You are right; I am going to talk to my mommy. I guess Anthony, you better call your mother and have her pick you up".

Anthony replied, "No, problem".

When Anthony's mother picks him up, she asked how did it go? Anthony acknowledged to Dee Jackson; Bernard tried to fix him up with somebody in his neighborhood. Those girls were more Bernard's type than mines. Dee Jackson told Anthony; I would have guessed because Bernard is two years older than you. Anthony was not ready to go home so; he requested for Dee Jackson to drive him over his cousin Carl house.

When Anthony got to his cousin Carl house, there was a girl name Denise standing in his driveway. Cousin Carl introduced him to Denise. Denise was slender, curvy shaped and had a delightful personality. Anthony greeted her hello and informed her; she was visiting a good guy. He let her know, Cousin Carl was the nicest guy a person could ever be friends with.

Carl replied, "Thanks Anthony but; unfortunately, Denise feels as if us are too different to be hanging out with each other".

Denise replied, "We are too different. I am looking for something else. I need me somebody, who is more my style. I need someone similar, as your cousin Anthony".

Carl replied, "If this is the case then, Denise you can have Anthony".

After this introduction, Anthony was confused. Cousin Carl did not get a chance to introduce him to any other girls in his neighborhood. Cousin Carl transferred Denise phone number over to Anthony; and they started talking on the phone. Denise was a pretty girl but; Anthony socializing with Denise made Carl depressed. Anthony did not feel comfortable socializing with Denise. Despite Denise feeling towards Carl, Carl enjoyed

Denise company. Anthony enjoyed Denise company too but; he felt ashamed of how they met. Anthony informed his mother of the situation and Dee Jackson did not like it either.

On Thanksgiving Day at the family dinner, Anthony invited Denise to come and participate at the event. Anthony was now fourteen years of age and had been knowing Denise for over a year. Anthony's cousin Carl was at the holiday dinner also. The doorbell rang, and Anthony answered the door. Denise walked in and gave Anthony a kiss on his cheek.

Dee Jackson replied, "Anthony can I see you in another room please. Anthony, is this Denise? You still dating Denise. I can tell you son, it's not right to date Carl's ex-friend. To tell you another thing; I do not like her. I can tell Denise is an opportunist. She thinks there are more benefits with you than your cousin Carl. This is wrong in my eyes because your cousin Carl has become depressed".

After that speech, Anthony knew what he had to do for obvious reasons. Anthony sat down and got both Denise and Carl together. He allowed them to discuss their differences out. It still did not help them become a couple but; it helped Anthony relieve his consciousness. Dee Jackson was pleased also. Denise stopped socializing with Anthony; and Anthony returned to his old self in search for another girlfriend. Anthony's mother Dee Jackson commented on his routine.

Dee Jackson replied, "Okay son, I have to tell you. Anthony, you are getting old and becoming a little man. I am going to call my best friend Stacy. I have wanted you to meet Stacy's daughters for a long time. Stacy has twins name Tracy and Lacy. She also has a daughter name Latonya and her youngest daughter's name Melody. The twins are one year older than you; and Karen is the same age as you. Melody is one year younger. The twins are in High School. Karen, I believe goes to your school and Mel stays with her grandparents. I am thinking, all these girls are still available to date".

## CHAPTER FOUR

# TWINS

Anthony thought for a second about twins. How can he pass up an opportunity to meet twins? Anthony did not think too much about the other daughters. He was just concentrating on the twins. Then, Anthony thought about what Cousin Bernard had advised him. Nobody wants their mother fixing them up on a date. Anthony at first notified his mother, he did not want to meet the twins. His mother introduced the twin's mother to him. Anthony thought Stacy looked like a beautiful queen. Stacy and Dee Jackson were the same age but, Stacy could pass for a college student. The idea entered Anthony mind, if these daughters resembled anything as their mother, then, he had no problems.

Stacy was nice and attractive to be her age. She thought; it would be a great ideal for Anthony to meet her daughters because the boys they were dating were troublemakers. Anthony believed; it was his obligation to meet her daughters. Stacy informed Anthony; she would be there tomorrow with all her daughters to introduce him. Stacy told him, she has sat down at the table and explained to her daughters; Dee Jackson has a son who is different. Dee Jackson's son is different because he is nice and shy. Anthony felt good, Stacy thought of him this way. His brother B.J always let him know he talked entirely too much.

The first time he met Stacy's daughters, they stared at him as if he was an exhibit in a zoo. The twins just laughed. Karen did not say a word; and the youngest daughter made a mean look on her face. The first person who spoke was the youngest daughter Melody.

Melody replied, "My mommy told me if I come and introduce myself to you, I can use the telephone to call my friend. Will you tell me, where your phone is located?"

Anthony replied, "The phone is in the kitchen beside the refrigerator".

Lacy and Tracy both stepped out of the car. They were good looking twins; they were identical sisters who could charm any hederal sexual man with one look. Anthony glanced at their body silhouettes and started to think with lust. He tried to say hello without looking in Lacy eyes. Lacy quickly responded with a smile.

Lacy replied, "My mother told me Anthony, you were cute. She is right; and you are shy too. Hey Tracy, he will not even look at you good. Anthony, don't you want to get a better look at us. How do we look?"

Anthony replied, "Alright, wow! Dressed alike and I cannot tell any difference between your sister and you. Stacy's twin daughters! I finally meet the most beautiful twins in Winston Salem, NC".

Lacy replied, "Anthony, you are a charmer. Hey Tracy, he is a charmer too. Tracy and me like charmers".

Anthony remembered; he had not spoken to their other sister yet. He looked at Latonya and she waved with a quick motion. There was something about Latonya that was strange. I guess because she was so reserved, unlike the other sisters. Latonya sort of reminded Anthony of himself. Anthony enjoyed a girl who was conservative. The twins immediately informed him, not to waste too much time with Latonya because she does not talk too much.

Anthony replied, "My mom would want everybody to come in the house because she feels we will be making a show case for the neighbors. Matter of fact, everybody can head down to the basement, where we do all the entertaining".

Immediately, the twins spoke in behalf of the other two sisters.

Tracy replied, "This is a wonderful idea Anthony, you are so smart".

Lacy replied, "They say, "what goes on in the basement, stays in the basement".

As everybody walked in the house and downstairs to the basement, Anthony began thinking. He thought; as nice as Stacy's daughters are, these girls can be intimidating. Anthony began to sweat with anxiety. The twins were too much for him to handle. Anthony figured; if he could spend time with only one daughter at a time and not all four daughters at a time, this would be his best option. This was his only option to making a love connection with any daughter. Anthony got a better look at Latonya. Latonya was as fine as the twins. Anthony tried to imagine, what an experienced man would do in a situation as this.

After everyone got comfortable downstairs, Lacy glared at Anthony.

Lacy replied, "Anthony, I bet you make out with your girlfriends down here".

Tracy replied, "I bet he does too. Anthony, my mother said you were nice but; do you make out with girls in the basement?"

Anthony debated the question in his mind for a second. He realized having a conversation with all the daughters was not going to be easy. Anthony tried to invent an answer which both daughters would be happy.

Anthony replied, "No, I don't make out with girls in my mom's house. My mother would kill me."

Lacy replied, "Do you always try to say or do the correct thing".

Anthony replied, "Yes, most of the time".

Tracy replied, "Good because we are going to play a little game".

Melody replied, "Oh no, not this game. I think I am going upstairs".

Tracy replied, "Latonya are you joining this game with your sisters".

Latonya replied, "I do not condone this game".

Lacy replied, "Tracy are you sure, you want to play this game".

Tracy replied, "Yes".

Lacy replied, "Tracy, you always play dirty".

Anthony is confused. He is wondering, what is about to happen.

Anthony replied, "Girls, what you all are thinking about now?"

Tracy replied, "Lacy and me are going to use the bathroom to discuss some things. We will be right back to ask you some questions".

The twins go to the bathroom and leave Latonya with Anthony. Anthony looks at Latonya for an answer for what is about to happen. Latonya is so quiet; Anthony could hear a pin drop on the floor. One of the twins come out the bathroom. Anthony is confused about which twin has come out, Lacy or Tracy. The twin girl sits beside Anthony.

Anthony replied, "Okay, is this Lacy or Tracy?"

Lacy replied, "Oh, you don't know who you talking to?"

Anthony replied, "No because you and your twin sister are dressed alike".

Lacy replied, "Well, try to remember Tracy is the mean one and she is smaller than me. Let me ask you. Who would you rather date, Tracy or me?"

Anthony replied, "I just met the both of you. Right now, I like the both of you".

Lacy replied, "Okay this is nice but; if you had to choose right now. Who would it be, Tracy or me?"

Anthony replied, "I do not know".

Lacy replied, "Alright then, if you want tell me, I am going to let you talk to Tracy".

After Lacy departed to retrieve Tracy, Anthony began to look at Latonya. Latonya shook her head left and right. Anthony could tell, Latonya was displeased with the twins. Latonya did not say a word to Anthony. Tracy walked into the room with a smile on her face.

Tracy replied, "Lacy told me you would not answer her question. Anthony, I just want to be truthful with you. If you pick me, I can go upstairs to tell my mother; and she would be happy. Then, we can all go out and celebrate at the movie theater. I am sure my mother would have no problems paying your way".

Anthony replied, "Tracy, it sounds good but; I cannot decide right now because I just met the both of you. It is not fair for me to make a decision so fast".

Tracy replied, "Okay, I am just going to tell you this. If you date Lacy, you are going to be disappointed. Lacy don't believe in having sex before marriage. No offence but; how are you going to drive a car unless you test drive it?"

Anthony replied, "Tracy, this is too much information to tell me".

Tracy replied, "Anthony, look into my eyes. I know you are not going to turn me down".

Anthony glanced at Latonya and Latonya glanced back.

Tracy replied, "Wait a minute. I do not believe, what I see".

Anthony replied, "What?".

Tracy replied, "Anthony, why are you looking at Latonya. Latonya has not opened her mouth, not one time. I think Anthony, you are liking my sister Latonya. Alright, I am telling Lacy. I am going to get her right now".

Anthony expression on his face was amazement. Latonya notified Anthony; he better taken care of this problem because she was not going home and arguing with her twin sisters. The twin sisters returned; and they had a serious look on their face.

Lacy replied, "Anthony, what is going on? You got eyes for Latonya".

Anthony replied, "No way! I was only trying to receive advice about this little game we are playing".

Tracy replied, "Oh, you think this is a game".

Lacy replied, "This is no game. We are trying to find out, who you want to date".

Anthony replied, "Tracy said, 'this is a game".

Tracy replied, "I told a lie; this is not a game. Anthony, who do you like the most and do not look at Latonya".

Anthony replied, "I told everybody, I like everyone. Right now, I like each person as a friend".

Lacy replied, "Okay Tracy, enough of this game. Nobody is getting anywhere with this. What we are going to do is invite Anthony to our house for dinner this weekend. When he comes and see us then, Anthony can decide. For the moment, let us go tell mother, we are tired. We will see Anthony, this weekend for dinner".

Later in the night, Anthony confided to his brother B.J. Anthony asked his brother, how girls expect a guy to choose a girlfriend, especially when they just meet each other?

B.J replied, "Little brother, you are thinking too much. Tell each daughter, you care about their feelings; and you do not want to hurt no one. But you say who ever prove to me, they want me the most will be my girlfriend".

Anthony replied, "Big brother, you are a genius. The only thing is, will the twins be upset if I tell them this".

B.J replied, "If the twins get upset, just say I don't know why girls like to play games, when guys are ready to prove their love at any time".

Anthony replied, "Boy, you are smart".

B.J replied, "Thank you. Now, Anthony go take control and handle them girls. I have given you great words of wisdom out the playboy's handbook. If you need more help, just let me know".

Anthony replied, "No big brother; I think, I am good now".

B.J replied, "Good".

The next day, Anthony was having anxiety attacks. He could not believe, how situations were making him nervous. Anthony talked to his friend, who was his classmate, Ricky. He told Ricky about the dinner meeting with the twins at their house. Ricky was overjoyed Anthony could be dating a twin. Ricky envisioned popularity in school, and he knew dating a twin would make Anthony popular in school. In return, Ricky notified all the classmates; Anthony was socializing with attractive twin girls. It turned out, it was the talk of the town, how Anthony was invited to dinner by some attractive twins and could be dating one of them. This was every schoolboy's dream and a trophy piece for dating excellence.

When Anthony told Ricky the names of the twins. Ricky already heard about them. Twins were no secrete around town, especially attractive twins. Ricky could not believe how lucky Anthony had become. This type of opportunity only came once. Anthony imagined himself being in the middle between Lacy and Tracy hugged up. Next, would come following is Latonya because she would be jealous and enraged. Yes, Latonya would want him too. Last, Melody would join forces, just to fit in with everybody else.

Anthony did not think of Melody in a sexual way. He figured; for no reason at all, I would be Melody boyfriend, just to make other guys upset. Another idea revealed in his mind, when all the girls in Winton Salem hears about him dating four sisters, all the girls will want to date him. Anthony pictured; he would be irresistible to any local girl his age in the area. This made Anthony sweat with anxiety. Anthony realized to get rid of the anxiety attacks, he needed to stop day dreaming. He stopped thinking about Stacy's daughters and concentrated on schoolwork.

The day before Stacy's dinner, Anthony's mother Dee Jackson notified him to dress casually. Dee Jackson made it clear, Stacy's dinner was nothing fancy so; please dress to be comfortable. The dinner was a gathering for fun and relaxation, after a week of work or school. Dee Jackson sent a message to Anthony. Stacy would be serving spaghetti and sweet peas for dinner. Dinner time was estimated to be at six o'clock so; they would leave at five o'clock.

During the day, Dee Jackson and Anthony left on time to Stacy's address. Stacy's house was only five minutes away from the neighborhood. She stayed in the same school district as my mom. Stacy's house was nice and clean on the inside. Instantly, Anthony noticed; he must be at the twin's house because he heard girls fussing from familiar voices in the background. Stacy shouts out in a loud voice, "Girls company has arrived".

Stacy replied, "Anthony, I do not know, what is taking them so long to come out and greet you but; walk down the hallway into the open foyer and have a seat".

Anthony replied, "Okay".

As Anthony sits in the recliner chair, he watches as the younger daughter came out a bedroom. First, Melody greeted with a wave as she passed him to the dining room. A couple of minutes later, Latonya came from downstairs. Latonya waves and whispers in a low voice, "God help you". Then, finally the twins appear together out their room. They both sit down in a love seat, right across from Anthony.

Tracy replied, "Good afternoon Anthony, it feels as if ages, since we saw you last. I know, it's only a week but; it feels longer. What do you think Lacy?"

Lacy replied, "I was just thinking the same thing. Anthony, I think you have grown in just a week's time".

Anthony replied, "I know, you all are twins but; it really amazed me, how the both of you think the same and look the same. Do the both of you dress the same all the time".

Lacy replied, "No, not all the time. Only when we wear clothes our mother bought us. The clothes we buy, when we shop for ourselves are not the same. It is mother, she thinks it is cute if we dress alike".

Anthony replied, "Kool, now which one of you is Lacy?"

Lacy replied, "I am Lacy, remember what I told you".

Anthony started observing how Lacy was just a fraction taller than Tracy. Tracy personality was a little meaner than her sister also. Anthony wondered how he could make Tracy a little upset to recognize her.

Anthony replied, "Tracy, I just happen to observe you are slightly, just slightly bigger than Lacy".

Tracy replied, "Anthony, I am not bigger than my sister. I cannot believe you said this to me. You really think I am bigger; what are you implicating?"

Anthony replied, "Calm down Tracy, I am not indicating anything. Your sister and you look the same; both of you are probable the same size".

Tracy replied, "You really think so Anthony".

Anthony replied, "Yes, I think both of you are fine. The both of you appear as if you could be beauty queens".

The twins blushed, while Latonya walks back into the foyer. Latonya examined everyone in the room with her eyes up and down.

Latonya replied, "Hey everyone in hear; mother says wash your hands. It is time to eat. Anthony the bathroom is to the left down the hallway".

Anthony replied, "Sure, thanks".

Lacy replied, "I hope, you are ready to choose between my sister and me. Who do you want to be your girlfriend?"

Tracy stands up and kiss Anthony on the right side of his face. Then, Lacy stands up and kiss Anthony on the left side of his face. Latonya shakes her head. Latonya grabs Anthony's hand and directs him by pointing towards the bathroom.

Latonya replied, "Tracy and Lacy, do not start nothing until after we eat. Anthony appetite is going to spoil. Anthony, please hurry up and wash your hands, where we can eat".

While Anthony was eating his dinner, his nerves were jumping everywhere. Anxiety and anxiousness started to take over Anthony's body. Then, suddenly Stacy's phone rang. It rang, rang and rang until Stacy answered the phone. I could hear displeasure in her voice.

Stacy replied, "Hello! Oh, you again. How many times, I must tell you; she doesn't except phone calls during dinner time".

Stacy hangs up the phone. She shakes her head and returns to the dinner table. Shortly after this, the phone rings again. Stacy leaves the table, answers the phone and takes the receiver off the hook.

Stacy replied, "Excuse me to everyone at the dinner table but; these teenagers keep calling for Tracy and Lacy. These teenagers do not know, what no means".

Dee Jackson replied, "I wished, I would get a phone call for Anthony. I guess, he is not at age, where he enjoys talking on the phone. Although the other son B.J, he stays on the phone. I should be grateful; if one does and the other don't".

Stacy replied, "Yes, you should be grateful because the twins have boys calling left and right".

After dinner the twins invited Anthony into the foyer to relax. Latonya follows right behind Anthony. Anthony could tell eating help his anxiety go away. Tracy started talking; while he was thinking about the phone calls the twins were receiving during dinner at their house.

Tracy replied, "I hope, you enjoyed dinner Anthony".

Anthony replied, "I did, it was good".

Lacy replied, "Our mother is a good cook".

Anthony replied, "Yes, she is good".

Lacy replied, "Anthony, who are you going to choose to date?"

Anthony replied, "Alright, I have decided. I have figured; since both of you have a lot of male friends, why not I stay friends. I date the both of you whenever."

At first Tracy did not say anything. Tracy glanced at Lacy. Lacy gave Anthony a mean look.

Anthony replied, "Okay, if this is not good then, whomever can prove they want me the most will be my girlfriend".

Tracy then, gave Anthony a mean look. Both the twin girls were looking mean at Anthony.

Anthony replied, "What is wrong with this?"

Latonya replied, "Anthony, have you lost your mind".

Stacy replied, "Okay Anthony, I do not know, who you have talked to. Furthermore, we do not swing like this".

Tracy replied, "Prove, we want you like you how? I know, you not talking about sex".

Lacy replied, "No, he cannot be talking about sex".

Latonya replied, "No, he didn't say anything about sex".

Tracy replied, "Yes, he is! He wants to have sex".

Lacy replied, "Anthony are you trying to have sex with one of us; or maybe you are trying to have sex with the both of us. If you are, I am going to tell your mother and mines also".

Anthony replied, "Oh no, I didn't say sex. Girls, there is a misunderstanding somewhere".

Tracy replied, "Okay, Anthony you want sex. If we give you sex, will you decide who you want to date then".

Anthony replied, "Okay, sure".

Tracy replied, "Then, notify us; when you want to do this. Between now and until you let us know; we want talk to you about dating anymore".

Anthony replied, "Okay".

Anthony and his mother departed Stacy house, and departed to their own residence. The five minutes of travel time on the road, allowed Anthony to evaluate, how bad his anxiety occurred over Stacy house. Anthony also thought, how he could possibly have sex with one of the twins. The idea made Anthony sweat in his mother passenger seat. Anthony's anxiety occurred; and he starts to get nervous.

Dee Jackson replied, "Anthony, what is wrong? You going to be okay. Wow! You are soaking wet. I see sweat pouring down your face. Stacy's pretty girls got you hot and bothered. I know this was a lot to handle, having dinner with all them pretty girls".

Anthony replied, "No mom, I am fine".

Anthony could not believe; his mom noticed he was nervous. He realized, if his mom could tell he was nervous then, the twins could tell too. Anthony figured the notion; if one of the twins is going to prove she wants him then, by having sex with him was brilliant. He could not believe; they fell for it. Although, the idea was great, he was still unconvinced they would go through with it. Stacy's daughters were smart; and he knew it. Anthony felt the daughters knew he was bluffing; and they had a trick stored up for him. He just had to be careful, not to fall for it.

Anthony was nervous, talking to the twins about anything sexual. The twins became his dream and aspiration. Anthony thought about them night and day. He realized; his dreams were bigger than himself. This was a job for his brother B.J. B.J experience got Anthony into this mess; and B.J is going to have to orchestrate this mess to get Anthony out. In the process, Anthony figured; the twins were orchestrating their own ideas. The twins could not believe Anthony had the nerve to talk about sex because he was only fourteen. Because of Anthony's age and background, the twins figured sex would be the last thing on his mind.

Lacy replied, "I am beginning to hate Anthony. Anthony is acting as one of them other boys, who is a sex maniac at school".

Tracy replied, "Lacy, you know he probable just want to have sex with us so; he can tell his friends, he had sex with twins".

Lacy replied, "This is all them boys think about".

Tracy replied, "I know, what we can do. We can try to get him to invite us over to his house because Anthony is alone at his home a lot. Then, we can see if he is a jerk and is serious about sex or he is just bluffing".

Latonya replied, "Why would you tease Anthony this way? Tracy, you are so mean. Anthony would never go through with something this way. Anthony is a nice boy. He is Dee Jackson's son and only fourteen. Couldn't you tell, how nervous Anthony was and talking about sex. I thought, Anthony was going to pass out because sweat was rolling down his face".

Lacy replied, "Well, he shouldn't insinuate".

Latonya replied, "I feel as if nobody should be pressuring anybody to choose, who they want to be with. Don't you know, boys cannot handle pressure".

Tracy replied, "No, Latonya and Lacy; Anthony needs a lesson. I say, we show up while he is alone at his house. If Anthony mentions anything about sex, we are done with him. Then, we go tell our mother".

Lacy replied, "This is fine with me".

Anthony receives a phone call from Tracy. Anthony answered the phone; and when he realized it was one of the twins, immediately he starts sweating and anxiety starts to build.

Anthony replied, "Hello, what's happening? How is everything going?"

Tracy replied, "This is Tracy, you have been thinking about us?"

Anthony replied, "Sure, I think about you all, all the time".

Tracy replied, “Anthony, when you get out of school, you are alone at home?”

Anthony replied, “Yes, my parents are separated so; my dad does not stay here anymore. B.J and my mom work during the daytime and come home late at night”.

Tracy replied, “You have it made. Pretty much, you can do whatever you want to at home or until someone comes home”.

Anthony replied, “Sure!”.

Tracy replied, “Is it alright, if you have company”.

Anthony replied, “Sure!”.

Tracy replied, "I am going to give the phone to Lacy”.

Lacy replied, “Anthony, normally my sister does not beat around the bush but; today she is shy. I am going to come out and tell you. If, you want to spend some time with us, we can meet you after school at your house while you are alone.”

Anthony replied, “Oh, can I think about it a little?”

Lacy replied, “What is there to think about. Have you changed you mind about sex?”

Anthony replied, “Sex, did you say sex! Oh no, I haven’t changed my mind about sex. I usually get home after school around three o’clock in the afternoon.

Lacy replied, “Anthony are you sure, you want to have sex?”

Anthony replied, “Sure, why I wouldn’t”.

Lacy replied, “Well, Tracy and I will be there tomorrow after school. I am going to put Tracy on the phone”.

Tracy replied, “Anthony, be ready because it is going to be something special”.

Anthony replied, “Sure, something special”.

When B.J returned home from work, Anthony confided to his brother; the twins were coming to the house after school. The twins wanted him to have sex with them. Anthony informed B.J; the advice he gave about the twins, proving if they really want him then to show it, had gotten him in this situation. So now, he was going to need some more advice to get out of the situation.

B.J replied, "Anthony, you got to be joking".

Anthony replied, "Nope, this is not a joke. What I need to do?"

B.J replied, "Anthony, do not worry. The twins do not want to have sex with you. They are trying to see, how far you are going to go. They know, your mother will kill you, if you have sex in this house. Do not worry; and why are you sweating. It looks as if you are having an anxiety attack".

Anthony replied, "I think so".

B.J looks at Anthony and starts to laugh. He tried to think about what to say in a sarcastic way to make his brother laugh.

B.J replied, "If the twins are thinking about sex, then, to be safe, hear is a box of condoms and a camera. Please have fun and take lots of pictures. I cannot believe my brother is going to get his first piece with twins".

Anthony replied, "B.J, you must be out of your mind. I am going to end this mess by tomorrow".

The next day, Anthony returned to school. He informed his friend Ricky; what was about to take place at his house after school.

Ricky replied, "Anthony are you sure, you don't need a backup or even a friend. There might be something which goes wrong or get out of hand".

Anthony replied, "No, I don't think so.

Ricky replied, "Anthony, do you think, you can really handle twins alone?"

Anthony replied, "You know, I do not know. Just in case, I will give you a phone call and tell you what I am doing".

Ricky replied, “This is a good idea. In between time, there is this pretty girl who has been looking for you. She said her name is Latonya”.

Anthony replied, “A girl name Latonya; show me where she is located”.

Ricky replied, “Sure, she is in the class on the bottom floor”.

Ricky escorts Anthony to the bottom floor where Latonya is located. The school hallway is filled with students walking up and down. Then, Latonya passes along and touches Anthony on the shoulder. Anthony turns around in astonishment.

Anthony replied, “Hey Ricky, this is the twin’s younger sister Latonya”.

Ricky replied, “Hello! What a beautiful girl you are”.

Latonya waved and then, smiled at Ricky. She pointed at Anthony; and then motion him with her finger to follow her down the hallway”.

Latonya replied, “Anthony, you know, you are in big trouble”.

Anthony replied, “How is this?”

Latonya replied, “I cannot believe, you are this stupid. My twin sisters are going to make a fool out of you. They are going to try and find out, if you are going to do something stupid as try to have sex with them. Then, if you do something stupid as try something sexual with them, they are going to tell my mother. On the other hand, if you do nothing, they will think you are weak. Therefore, you not going to win”.

Anthony replied, “Latonya, you got to be joking”.

Latonya replied, “Nope, I wish I was”.

Anthony replied, “They the ones who brought it up. I really don’t want sex; I have plenty of time for sex because I am only age fourteen”.

Latonya replied, “Well, you better do something quick”.

Anthony replied, “What can I do?”

Latonya replied, “There is nothing, I can do because I want see them until I get home”.

Anthony replied, “Latonya walks home with me. We can meet up with your sisters at my house”.

Latonya replied, “I know, I will get in trouble for doing this but okay”.

Latonya and Anthony decided to walk to Anthony’s house to meet the twins. They communicated about his interest in the twins. Latonya informed him; the twins’ interest in him was, he was nice. They wanted him to choose because Lacy thought he was a keeper; and Tracy, she was just being possessive. Tracy thought he was cute first. Overall, the twins’ ideas were pure platonic.

When Latonya and Anthony arrived at Anthony’s house they waited outside until the twins arrived. The twins arrived about thirty minutes after three. Latonya hid behind the house as Anthony escorted the twins into the house. While Anthony opened the door, the twins appeared to be confident but cautious of their surroundings.

Tracy replied, “Anthony are you sure, you have the house all alone?”

Anthony replied, “I am sure, we are all alone”.

Lacy replied, “Anthony, you are not afraid, are you?”

Anthony replied, “No, I am fine. Unless, you girls are thinking about doing something bad to me”.

Lacy replied, “What you think, we are going to do?”

Anthony replied, “I don’t know”.

Tracy replied, “Okay, I am going to stop the play stuff. Excuse me everyone but; what were you saying Anthony about proving ourselves to you”.

Anthony replied, "Oh, I just said. If you want me then, prove it".

Lacy replied, "I thought, you do not make out in your mom's house".

Anthony replied, "I don't".

Tracy replied, "Yes, right. If you want to make out, we can go into your bedroom".

Anthony is beginning to get worried; the conversation is activating his anxiety. He didn't imagine it to play out this way. Anthony wished Latonya would come on in the house and help him out. He knew, he had left the door unlock. He wondered, what was taking Latonya so long to come inside the house. Lacy was wondering; what in the world, Tracy was doing. Tracy and she had rehearsed this scene repeatedly. What Tracy was doing now, was not part of the rehearsal.

Lacy replied, "I am not going into no bedroom Tracy".

Tracy replied, "I told you, Anthony; Lacy is a scared kitten. I will prove my love to you and then, we can be a couple. Lacy, you stay here. Anthony and I are going to have fun in his bedroom for a little while. Give us a few minutes".

Lacy replied, "Tracy, I am tired of this. You disappear with boys all the time".

Tracy replied, "Okay Anthony, I am ready to go to your bedroom".

Anthony starts to have anxiety. Finally, Latonya comes into the house and into the bedroom. Latonya finds Tracy lifting her top up and exposing herself. Lacy is in the background watching with her hand over her mouth.

Latonya replied, "Tracy, what are you doing?"

CHAPTER FIVE

# SCHOOL TRANSFER

Tracy replied, "Oh Latonya, what are you doing here. Lacy and I are just teasing Anthony. I know, you don't believe; I was going to actually have sex with Anthony".

Lacy replied, "I was teasing Anthony. I was doing nothing".

Latonya replied, "I am going to tell mommy".

Just when Latonya mention mommy, we heard a car horn. There was a car waiting in the driveway with two high school boys. Lacy announced to her sisters, let's go because our ride home is out here. The girls walked outside; and Anthony noticed Tracy kissing some boy behind the steering wheel of the vehicle. Later, Anthony found out through Latonya, the twins were on a date the same day with the two high school boys in the vehicle. Anthony informed his classmate Ricky, the entire story. In return, Ricky tried to date Tracy also. Tracy told Ricky, she would only go out with Anthony and not one of his flunky friends".

Anthony figured; why pursue Tracy on a date. The only reason, Tracy wanted him is because she didn't want him to go out on a date with Lacy. Lacy didn't want to pursue Anthony because she didn't want to make Tracy jealous. She knew, if Tracy got jealous, Tracy would have sex with Anthony. In the event, the entire relationship for everybody ended. Anthony was back at searching for another girl to be his girlfriend.

Anthony informed his brother of the entire story on the twins. B.J felt sorry and disappointed; Anthony was not dating somebody.

B.J replied, "I am going to fix you up on a date. A nice pretty girl who will give you a good time, is what you need".

Anthony replied, "No, no thanks. I am fine. I can fix myself up. I don't need, nobody fixing me up. Besides, I don't want just sex, I want a girlfriend".

B.J replied, "I understand what you need, what you need is some sex. Right now, you feel lonely and horny. You are going to high school this year. It is time for you to become a man and quit acting as a child".

Anthony replied, "I do not act as a child".

B.J replied, "You are still a virgin, right. Well then, you are still acting as a child".

Anthony thought about what B.J had said. He did not believe; he was acting as a child anymore because Tracy, who is a twin, tried to have sex with him. B.J taught him the magic words to get a girl to have sex. If a girl thought; she had interest in him, Anthony would tell her to prove it and then, she would have sex with him. Experience taught Anthony, it worked on Tracy; and she was smart so, it would work on any girl. Anthony figured; it would have worked on Lacy or Latonya. These words were magic, straight out of the playboy book, as B.J informed him.

One day, B.J tried to get Anthony to have sex with one of his girlfriends. B.J bribed the girl to have sex with Anthony, by telling her he would take her on an exclusive date alone another time. The events of the date were B.J informed Anthony; a girl he knew owed him two movie tickets. The only way he was going to collect, he had to show two people needed tickets. He notified her; his little brother and I needed tickets to go to the movies. Anthony had to tag along to receive the second ticket. At first, Anthony turns down the invitation. Later, Anthony realized; his mother Dee Jackson made plans to go out with someone, and she was going to be out late.

Anthony did not want to be at home alone. He decided to go out with his brother B.J. Anthony notified B.J of his decision; and B.J was compliant. B.J entire idea was falling in place. During the duration of the date, Anthony felt as a third wheel. Anthony prayed; the date would end after the movies, and B.J would take the girl back home. Anthony was unlucky; after the movies they travel a short distance to a park, where it was dark and abandon.

B.J replied, "I guess Anthony, you probably wondering, why we wanted you to tag along.

Anthony replied, "It did cross my mind, sort of".

B.J replied, "You are right; we have a surprise for you. The surprise is not just the movies. I want you to make out with my friend".

Anthony replied, "Why, isn't this what you are supposed to do".

B.J replied, "Well you right, but tonight she is for you".

Anthony replied, "What the heck, you are talking about".

B.J friend replied, "Anthony, do not get excited because it is your first-time having sex. Nobody is going to know about this but, us and you.

Anthony replied, "No way, I can find my own girlfriend to have sex with".

B.J replied, "Little brother, I need to tell you something. I am leaving home and joining the Navy. I want to make sure; you are set straight".

Anthony replied, "Okay, but I am straight. What! You are joining the Navy? You sure you want to do this".

B.J replied, "I am definitely positive. Which is why, this is my first and last time to try to hook you up with someone".

Anthony replied, "Thanks, I really do appreciate it. I am leaving also. I am transferring to another school district. I asked mom, can I stay with our grandparents for a while".

B.J replied, "No, no way! You are going to leave this nice basement; what we entertained the girls with. Also, where you could have made out with the twins. In addition, we are going to leave mommy all alone".

Anthony replied, "Well, I am afraid it's true because it doesn't seem, as if she is going to get back with dad. Maybe this will make me a respectable guy because I want to find a respectable girl. Not someone who knows; I have my mother's house alone, where I can make out".

B.J replied, "I wish you good luck brother".

When Anthony started school over his grandparents' house, it was totally different. Everything was structured and organized. Anthony's grandparents operated their life on a tight routine. His grandparents trained Anthony on what time breakfast was set at the table, what time to be at the table for lunch and dinner. One thing for sure, the food was always good and on time. Anthony did not have to worry about chores, only he had to make sure his homework was done and correct. Anthony enjoyed the lifestyle because there was no pressure from sex or anything.

The students at his school appeared to live more at eased and civilized than where his mother stayed. They were not competing as much for dates; and he could tell the tension in the classroom was less. Anthony walked from class to class; and he did not see one student doing anything out the normal. He was really impressed about how the students operated. Anthony felt as if he was living the good life. Slow moving was his goal.

Anthony figured; the girls looked as if they were so nice and friendly.

This one girl for instance, her name was Sabrina Robinson, who attended his school and live around the corner from him. Anthony thought; she looks innocent, I will talk to her because she appeared to be lonely. He had not introduced himself to any girls in the area. Also, if he wanted to visit her, she was in walking distance. One day she was standing on the bus stop; and he introduced himself. Sabrina watched him get on the bus. She followed behind him and started asking him questions. Sabrina wanted to know, where he lived; how long had he been living there and who he socialized with. It was amusing to Anthony because he was a frequent visitor of the area, when he visited his grandparents. Sabrina's problem was why; she never met Anthony before.

Anthony had a guy friend in the area named Robert. He grew up with his friend named Robert. He just never thought about going to school over his grandparents' house until then. Furthermore, Anthony never thought about dating a girl over to his grandparents' house. Sabrina figured; he was a new person in the area. She was so excited about meeting someone new in the area because she was tired of the guys which already existed.

The relationship Anthony built with Sabrina was pleasant in the beginning. Sabrina and Anthony would talk on the bus and discuss schoolwork. Then, one day there was a new bus driver, who was driving the route. Instead of transporting students to the right bus stop, the bus driver delivered students to their residence. Finally, it was Sabrina and Anthony left on the bus. Sabrina announced to the driver, take me home next. When Sabrina finished directing the bus driver to her house, Anthony was relieved. She politely asked Anthony, "Do you want to come to my house and watch some T.V".

Anthony thought at first against it but; he reconsidered because it might be impolite to turn down an invitation from a new friend. Anthony informed her, just a little while would be fine and slowly exited the bus behind Sabrina. When they arrived at Sabrina's house, his nerves automatically started jumping. He could feel his anxiety coming out. As Anthony looked at Sabrina, it appeared she was a little nervous also. Anthony told her, she had a lovely home and he would see her tomorrow. Then, as he reached for the exit door, she tries to comfort him by saying she is alone, and her parents will not be home until late. Will he stay just a little longer?

Anthony could not believe; she would inform him of this. He wished she had kept this information to herself. Now, he felt obligated to stay with her a little longer.

Anthony replied, "Sabrina, you are a nice person. I do not think, I should be alone with you".

Sabrina replied, "It is just my mother and me alone in this house. I am sure, she wouldn't mind if I have company for a little while, until she arrives".

Anthony replied, "What about guys?"

Sabrina replied, "If my mother comes home, I will tell her we are studying schoolwork. This is what we do anyways. Anthony, you can stop by my house after school and study anytime you want to. I will notify my mother, you will be here studying and keeping me company, while she is at work".

Anthony replied, "Sabrina, you sure you want to do this?"

Sabrina replied, "Yes, because I like you; and I want my mother to meet you. It would be nice, if we could study tomorrow, where she can meet you".

Anthony replied, "I guess, it would be fine".

Anthony thought the rest of the night, after he left Sabrina's house. He meets Sabrina's mother; and he figured this was a little too fast. Anthony was hoping Sabrina and he could take things a little slower. He was not in a rush to get in a relationship with Sabrina because Anthony was new to the school district. Anthony knew if he got into a serious relationship with Sabrina, looking at other girls would end; and it have not even begun. He thought there was one girl, who was fine. This girl's name was Tammy B. He had eyes for her; and she went to his school. Anthony thought, if he could get her attention, he would not look at Sabrina again. Tammy B was the prettiest girl, he had ever seen.

Tammy B was a girl who resemble a black Maryland Monroe, who was a famous Actress. She had a shape which was voluptuous; and her mere presence gave Anthony the shakes. Tammy had a mole on her right cheek below her right eye. Anthony thought, it was so attractive. When he talked to other guys about her, those guys wondered was his mind cloudy; did he have bad judgement or maybe he was just prejudice to other girls. Tammy had a personality; she believed no other girls were pretty except her. The other guys did admit eventually; yes, she was pretty. Although, she was not the only pretty girl in school.

Some guys tried to tell Tammy; she was below average looking. Anthony figured; guys were saying this to bring Tammy down to their level so, they could try to talk to her better. Tammy was very stuck on herself; and she was not shy expressing it either. It was a big turn on to Anthony. The only problem, Anthony had was Tammy did not know Anthony existed. On the alternative side, Sabrina was totally different. On some moments, Sabrina treated Anthony like she was possessive.

In addition, Sabrina wanted public affection and expected for Anthony to be loyal to her desires. Sabrina could not stand Anthony telling her no. She wanted all of Anthony's attention and eventually, introduced Anthony to her mother. Sabrina already had informed her mother; Anthony is going to be her new boyfriend. Sabrina mother was very nice and kind. She told Anthony; she was glad, Sabrina had met a nice guy. Sabrina persuaded her mother to trust Anthony because he stayed around the corner; and she knew his grandparents.

Sabrina replied, "Mother, you do not have to worry about Anthony. You can walk to his grandparents' house where he lives".

Sabrina's mother replied, "You are talking about the elderly couple who has been living around the corner for years. I know who you are talking about because they have a nice garden".

Sabrina replied, "You are correct mother".

Sabrina mother replied, "I wonder can they give me a class on growing a garden. Sure, I trust that boy. Tell him to tell his parents hello".

Anthony enjoyed spending time with Sabrina most of the time but; he was not ready to become a boyfriend to Sabrina. It was terrible to be in a relationship at the beginning of the school year. Everybody Anthony thought, knew of this. There were so many interesting girls at his school. The relationship between Sabrina and Anthony got serious quickly. After Anthony met Sabrina's mother his life started to change.

One day, while Anthony and Sabrina were on the bus, Sabrina asked what was his clothes size? Anthony told her his size. The next day on the bus, Sabrina had a Sears bag from Hanes Mall. She told him to look in the bag. Anthony looked in the bag; and he found an expensive polo shirt and pants. He could not believe his eyes. Anthony had known Sabrina now, about only two months. He realized; his relationship with Sabrina had grown entirely too fast to soon. Anthony did not want to lead Sabrina on, no more. He believed; he had to put the relationship at an end, before somebody really got hurt.

Anthony replied, "Thanks for the clothes but; I have no money to buy you anything in return. Also, we only have known each other for a short time. It is not right for you to buy me clothes".

Sabrina replied, "It is fine. I bought you these clothes to celebrate our two months' anniversary. In addition, my mother will be out of town Saturday. I figured; we can have some alone time to ourselves to be romantic".

Anthony replied, "This idea you are plotting; it is going to get you in trouble".

Sabrina replied, "I thought you cared for me. What do you care, if I get in trouble? I want to make love to you. You, don't want me too? If you do, why don't you prove it to me, how much you want me? I am believing, when I introduced you to my mother, it was a bad idea".

Anthony replied, "Alright Sabrina, I will be there on Saturday. In return, I want you to take those clothes back to the mall".

Anthony imagined the entire day before Saturday, how things would play out. He figured; something bad was sure to happen before any sex would take place. Anthony decided; he would pretend he wanted sex with Sabrina to stay friends with her. But overall, he prayed Sabrina would be scared to have sex with anyone. The idea of Sabrina given him an invitation to have sex. Anthony could not understand, her bringing something up as this. Sabrina used the quote, "prove how much you want me", Anthony thought; he was the one to use this line. He laughed to himself, as if he was surprised, caught off guard and shocked. The words worked perfectly; and Sabrina knew how to persuade Anthony.

When Saturday arrived, Sabrina called Anthony on the phone early in the morning for him to report to her house. Anthony had no problems; he was cool and calm. He didn't even have anxiety. Anthony believed; everything would be all right and things would work itself out. Most guys, especially in the neighborhood, would beg at a chance as this. Sabrina was an attractive girl in the area. Anthony liked Sabrina but; his heart was with Tammy B. He wished, he could make love to Tammy B.

After Anthony arrived at Sabrina's house, he was amazed at himself because he was still calm. Anthony tried to picture all the possible scenarios of an outcome. All appeared to be pretty good, except for one. The scenario, where his hormones go into overdrive; and he cannot control himself for sex. Anthony thought, if Sabrina undresses in front of him, he is going to lose control. He hoped nothing as this would happen; and he keep his composer.

Sabrina invited Anthony into her house cautiously. When she opened the front door, she looked in all directions before allowing Anthony to enter. Sabrina made sure Anthony was alone. Anthony could tell probably; Sabrina had cleaned because he could smell the pine and bleach scent from a distance away. Sabrina quickly, started asking questions.

Sabrina replied, "What took you so long? I have been waiting for you".

Anthony replied, "The walk from my house to yours was a good distance far away. It gave me some time to think".

Sabrina replied, "Okay, this is good. We can sit on the sofa and talk. I want you to know, I don't want to make love with anybody but you. This is my first-time making love; I want to start slow".

Anthony replied, "Sabrina, I have to tell you; how nice you are to me. You do not have to rush to make love for anyone".

Sabrina replied, "Okay, lay on top of me so; we can cuddle".

Anthony figured; this will be fine. He could enjoy this because there was nobody undressing; and a little sex teasing don't hurt anybody. Anthony tried to remember, what his brother told him if he was given fore play to a girl. B.J told him to grab the girl hips, while laying on top of her; and rotate your hips in a circular motion. They called this grinding. Sabrina laid on the couch on her back and Anthony laid on top of her and started grinding. Sabrina began to make noises.

Anthony replied, "Sabrina are you okay! I am not hurting you, am I?

Sabrina replied, "No, No! Anthony, please don't stop. I feel good, keep going.

Anthony replied, "Okay, this is wonderful; how I am making out with you. I can do this, while we are kissing and everything for maybe one hour. After this, I am tired; and I have to go home".

One hour passed away; Anthony body begins to cramp up from all the twisting and turning on the sofa. Sabrina motions him to the bedroom. She stands up and points her finger to the room. Anthony stands up and begins to feel anxiety. He realized; Sabrina is informing him she wants sex.

Sabrina replied, "Anthony, you want to undress and lay in bed".

Anthony replied, "Sabrina, maybe some other time".

Sabrina replied, "No, what is the matter baby?"

Anthony replied, "I don't feel good. I think, I threw my back out on the sofa. Besides, I am all sweaty, sticky and need to take a bath".

Sabrina replied, “Well! We are going to have sex, now? I want you to be my baby daddy so bad”.

Anthony replied, “A baby, where did this come from? I am not trying to have a baby. I am too young to be having children”.

Sabrina replied, “Anthony, do not worry. Some of my girlfriends have babies. I wouldn’t ask you to take care of it.

Anthony replied, “I am not worried because it’s not going to be a baby”.

Sabrina replied, “Okay, but if we make love. I might become pregnant”.

Anthony replied, “Sabrina, I think you have a problem. How about we stay just friends. When, I see you; we are just friends and not dating”.

## CHAPTER SIX

# TAMMY

Sabrina replied, “Alright, you are going to break up with me because you scared to make love to me. You think, you are going to get me pregnant. You don’t even know, how to make love”.

Anthony replied, “Alright Sabrina, if you feel this way. I am going home”.

Sabrina replied, “Okay Anthony, you go ahead and leave”.

Later the next day, Anthony did not call Sabrina. The scene of Sabrina and Anthony making love or Anthony impregnating Sabrina kept playing in his mind. Anthony wondered how; he almost made the biggest mistake in his life. He could have become a daddy. It was a fact, Sabrina tried to trick him. Anthony could not trust Sabrina anymore. Anthony had the notion, not to ever talk to Sabrina ever again. Besides, he had feelings for another girl anyways. Anthony figured; this was the sign, he needed to move on and try to get close to Tammy B.

One week passed, Anthony had no dealings with Sabrina. He dodged Sabrina, while catching a ride with his friend next door to school. Anthony next door neighbor was named Robert. Robert was one grade higher and always gave Anthony advice, when he asked for it.

Robert replied, “Hey Anthony, I could have told you, Sabrina is weird. No brother in his right mind, would want to be trapped to take care of a baby. I could have told you; the girl has issues. Sabrina has issues with her mother, herself and you. She is trying to become somebody else, rather than live her normal life. I would gladly take you to school so; you want have to see Sabrina".

Anthony replied, "Thanks, so how long did it take you to get driver's license? I want to get my driver's license, when I turn sixteen".

Robert replied, "This is when I obtained my driver's license. I got my driver's permit, when I was fifteen; and then, I got my driver's license at sixteen".

Anthony replied, "Robert, can you train me to obtain my driver's permit?"

Robert replied, "Sure, but the best way to get your permit is sign up for driver's education class. I know, Tammy B is signing up for the class also.

Anthony replied," Why did you mention Tammy B?"

Robert replied, "I know, you have a crush on Tammy B. A lot of guys do. Although, they don't want to admit it".

Anthony replied, "Right! I wish, I had a chance to get to know her".

Robert replied, "Take the class, get your permit; and you will have a better chance of getting to know her".

Robert laughs and Anthony wonders, what is so funny.

Robert replied, "Tammy is looking for a boyfriend, who can drive someone and can take her out on a date.  Someone who don't have to be chaperon. This is important to a girl as Tammy".

Anthony replied, "I will keep that in mind".

Later during the year, Anthony signed his name on the list for driver's education. He continued riding to school with Robert. Four months passed; and it was December. The school had a Christmas party; and Sabrina notified Anthony, to invite him to attend the party with her. Anthony declined to attend; and Sabrina became irate.

Sabrina replied, "Anthony, I thought we had a good thing together. Where did we go wrong? Is it still a chance, we can get back together again? How about we go to the Christmas party together and make things like old times?"

Anthony replied, "I don't think so. I would like as if we be friends".

Sabrina replied, "My mother asked about you on occasions. She replied, "I let all the good guys go".

Anthony had no comment for what she said. He felt sad, but relieved the relationship was finally coming to an end. This was the first time, Anthony had to end a relationship with someone. Anthony had a girlfriend in school for two months; and he began to reflect feelings for Sabrina. Sabrina did buy him clothes. Although, Anthony did not except the clothes; it was special she did this. Albeit, becoming a baby's daddy was absurd. No doubt about it; Sabrina had to go. Anthony continues looking for a girlfriend; he wanted and desired female companionship. Having a baby was going too far.

After Christmas and New year, Anthony could not wait to start over a fresh new year. Driver's education class started in the month of March and ended at the end of the school year. The road training began right after this. Anthony turned fifteen in May so; he was motivated to learn. Tammy B was in his class; and she was perky with a beautiful smile. Anthony could not resist looking at her. When she walked past him, he felt anxiety. There was a guy in class who told Tammy B, Anthony is always looking at you. Anthony must have a crush on you. Tammy B, why not you and Anthony go on a date sometime.

Tammy B replied, "Why not Anthony asks me himself".

Anthony replied, "Tammy do you want to go out sometime".

Tammy B replied, "I do not go out with anybody. If I go out on a date, my date must pick me up in a nice car and we must do something nice. None of his friends can come because people talk too much. Yes, I would go out with you, Anthony. Whenever, you finish the class and get your driver's license. If this happens, you can take me out then".

Anthony was so excited; he did not know what to do. He called and notified his mother on the phone.

Anthony replied, "Hey mom, "I am taking this driver's education class in school. I am doing good in class; and I am making good grades in school. I am hoping to complete driver's education class in a month. Then, I will attempt to pass the road training, after the school year. If agreed, will you sign the form for me to obtain a driver's permit.

Dee Jackson replied, "Why you want to drive so young? You are only going on fifteen; and you are staying with your grandparents, who takes you where you have to go, including myself occasional".

Anthony replied, "Yes, right mom. I will turn fifteen in May; and it is the tradition in school to get your permit, when you turn fifteen".

Dee Jackson replied, "Anyways, I am planning for your birthday. What would you like to have?"

Anthony replied, "For you mom, my wish is to go to the Department of Motor Vehicles and for you to sign the form for me to receive my driver's permit".

Dee Jackson replied, "Okay, I see you are persistent about this idea. I will do this for you; and what else do you want".

Anthony replied, "I would like to pick up my friend Tammy B on a Saturday in the daylight because this is the only time, I am allowed to drive alone".

Dee Jackson replied, "Son, you are asking a lot here. I will see, what I can do. Hold up, I must allow you to drive my car! This is not going to be easy".

Anthony replied, "I know mom, I promise to be safe".

On the day Anthony turned fifteen, all his invites arrived at his birthday party. Anthony was able to pass his driver's education class and receive his driver's permit. The only requirement, which was left to obtain was his driver's license, after he passed the road class in school. He had to pass the driver's license test at the Department of Motor Vehicles, when he turned sixteen. Anthony would have to wait another year for his driver's license but, he had his driver's permit. He asked his mother for the keys to her vehicle (a new model Ford /Taurus car) so; he could pick up Tammy B. Dee Jackson agreed but; Anthony heard a lecture on things to do in case of an emergency. Tammy did not want Anthony to pick her up at her home address. She was very private about where she lived. Anthony did not mine, if she was private because he was just happy dating a fine girl as Tammy B. He imagined; she had to be cautious if she was a fine girl as this.

Anthony was proud of himself; it took courage for him to convince Tammy B to go out with him. He had to explain; it was his birthday. Anthony would be in his mom brand new vehicle. Also, he had the privilege to drive alone; and Tammy B enjoyed this. The only problem during the time, he was disappointed his brother was in the Navy and would not be there. Anthony pictured his brother becoming proud of him because he finally influenced a pretty girl to go on a date with him. Tammy B. waited at a designated area for Anthony to pick her up.

Anthony was on time, just as Tammy B demanded. Tammy B. sat in the vehicle and smiled. Anthony could tell, Tammy was flirting with him; and he started to get nervous. The first thing which came to Anthony's mind, he wanted to find a secluded place and make out. But he remembered, he had a house full of invites, family, and others waiting on him for his birthday. Anthony had to show Tammy B, his mom and himself included; he was professional. Tammy asked him, is his driving getting better since driver's education class. Anthony notified her; it is getting better every day.

Anthony arrived at his house and parked the automobile in the driveway. Tammy stared right into his eyes and told him, before we go inside, let's wait for a minute.

Tammy replied, "I can tell by the look outside, your birthday party is rocking. Even though, I need something to make me feel good".

Anthony replied, "I have to think a minute. What are you talking about?"

Tammy replied, "If you do not have anything, I can call and get us something".

Anthony replied, "You are talking about a drink and maybe something to smoke; or I hope, maybe a little sex".

Tammy replied, "All this is good but; yes, I am talking about a drink and something to smoke. The sex can come later".

Anthony replied, "I have no alcohol or nothing to smoke".

Tammy B replied, "Anthony, don't worry everything is cool. You go inside and keep you family occupied; I will use your mother car and get the stuff we really need to have fun. I am sure, your mother is looking for you know. Remember, I have my permit too so; it will not be a problem".

Anthony could not think clearly. He wanted to give Tammy B a good time; and this was the only thing on his mind. Anthony figured; Tammy will be safe with his mother's car; and she will come back quickly. He entered his mother's house to show, he made it back safely. After fifteen minutes past, there were questions.

Dee Jackson replied, "Where is your friend Tammy?"

Anthony replied, "Oh, she will be here".

Dee Jackson replied, "You supposed to have pick her up".

Anthony replied, "Right, I have to tell you. Tammy had to leave for a short time. She will be back".

Dee Jackson replied, "Okay, where are my keys. I need my keys to my vehicle".

Anthony replied, "Mom, I have to tell you. Tammy borrowed the car to pick something up. It was something, she had to have".

Dee Jackson replied, "Anthony, how could you! You just allowed a perfectly strange girl to borrow my car".

Anthony replied, "Tammy is not a stranger. She is my friend".

Dee Jackson replied, "How long has she been gone".

Anthony replied, "It is going on thirty minutes now".

Anthony was so embarrassed; he could not have a fun time with the rest of the invites. He was so worried about Tammy. He looked at his watch; and two hours had passed. Dee Jackson tried to file a stolen vehicle report. The police officer informed; there was nothing he could do because Anthony voluntary gave the car to Tammy. When three hours past, finally Tammy notified Anthony on the phone; she was returning to the house. Tammy told Anthony, she had drove to the mall to meet this guy; and he promised to buy alcohol and drugs for money. In the process, he had Tammy all over town going place to place.

Anthony realized; Tammy was fine. Although perhaps, he had to venture somewhere else. Tammy B. was too reckless for him. She wanted them drugs and not him. Tammy B. would do anything to get her favorite narcotics. The incident at Anthony's birthday party, caused Anthony's mother to prohibit him from dating Tammy B. At one time, he thought about given it another try because she was very pretty. When Anthony entered his tenth grade in school, Robert his friend, made a comment about Tammy which was disturbing.

Robert replied, "Anthony, how long have I been chauffeuring you to school. I believe; you owe me because you don't give me gas money. Just set me up with your friend Tammy B because you are not doing anything with her".

Anthony replied, "I don't care; she is just a friend".

Robert replied, "She is not only your friend, she is everybody's friend. I heard Anthony, you took her over to your mom's house; and she stole your mother's car. What fool would allow a dope head who prostitute for drugs to steal his mother's car".

Anthony replied, "You are a mother fucking liar; and I dare for you to say this to my face".

.

CHAPTER SEVEN

# ANTHONY RETURNS HOME

Robert proceeded to get in Anthony's face. Anthony and he commenced to fighting then, Robert brother separated them both. Robert banned Anthony from riding in his car. The next day, Anthony finds Robert at his school, kissing Tammy after class. Anthony felt; as if he had been betrayed. He was about to befriend Tammy again, until she displayed a show of affection for Robert. Now Anthony realized; Robert was close or somewhat accurate when informing him, Tammy only cares about drugs and herself. Tammy barely new Robert. Although, Robert had his own vehicle; and she needed him for connections to her drugs.

Anthony regretted having a friendship with Robert and Tammy B. Tammy tried to erase problems by implying, Robert and she were just acquaintances. She claimed, Robert had helped her in times of trouble. But this knowledge made the situation worst. Anthony had no one to socialize with and was lonely. He started feeling depressed and stayed anti-social. Anthony decided after the school year, he would return to his mother's home and live there as planned.

Dee Jackson replied, "Anthony, I am glad; you have made a decision of returning to me". Now, I can take care of you better, while you are under my roof. I am going to help you get a part time job and get you some transportation.

Anthony was so happy. This made him motivated to move back home. Anthony lived away from home for two years. It appeared to be a lifetime. Alisa across the street, met him at the mailbox and inspected him up and down.

Alisa replied, “Where have you been hiding? You have changed. You have grown taller. Where have you disappeared”.

Anthony replied, “I stayed with my grandparents to get a break from home. But I am back for good now. You know my brother is gone to the Navy”.

Alisa replied, “Yes, how does it feel to be the only son now?”

Anthony replied, “I feel a little different now”.

Alisa replied, “You know what, two years have passed; and Julie is still asking about you. Julie wants to know, where have you been living?”

Anthony replied, “Tell her, I had moved out of town”.

Alisa replied, “You know, she wants to see you”.

Anthony replied, “I already know”.

When Anthony transferred school, back to his home school district, it was different. The people he knew had grew. Most of the guys he knew, had grown taller, a lot taller than him. Anthony’s friend Ricky was not playing sports anymore. Ricky gave up becoming an athlete because he was now strictly a businessman and a so-called ladies man. Ricky wore church suits to school and sold jewelry after school every day. Anthony assumed; Ricky had grown at least six inches.

Ricky replied, “Hello, Anthony. Long time no see, short stuff”.

Anthony replied, “Look at you. You are tall and looking GQ”.

Ricky replied, “Right but I had to leave the sports alone. It got to ruff on me. I had to save my energy for the business and my girlfriends”.

Anthony replied, “Cool, I wish I was lucky as you and had a job”.

Ricky replied, “Anthony, you are still the lover boy. I am not going to forget. You dated them twins. You are keeping in contact with them”.

Anthony replied, “No, not anymore. I mean, I hear from their mother, through my mother. But no, I left them alone, when I moved to another school district. I am trying to upgrade”.

Ricky replied, “Upgrade from them, well good luck. I see the twins in school. They still will not give me a chance. They are some stuck up girls; and your friend Alisa too. I do not know, how you can upgrade from them”.

Anthony replied, “I just continue own being me”.

Ricky replied, “You haven’t changed a bit. You are still a player”.

Anthony decided the best way to attract the girl of his dreams, was to work and get a car as his friend Ricky. To get a job, Anthony had to find a job which was hiring. Anthony’s mother was asking about employment to help Anthony out from her friends. Anthony began gathering information from word of mouth from school. Anthony was now a junior in the eleventh grade and began to feel pressured to grow up. All his classmates appeared to be doing adult things with their lives; and he wanted to do the same.

One day, Ricky his classmate, advised Anthony to take a class called Vocational Occupation. The class assisted individuals with obtaining a job. Anthony signed up for the class. His teacher game him a piece of paper to show companies, he was a student who needed to work for a business to get credit for school. In return, he would work at a reduced price in good faith, while work he provided would be standard or above average work. The student would work during certain hours after school. Anthony notified his mom; what he was doing. She took the piece of paper and gave it to her boyfriend, who worked at Red Lobster. The job was perfect for Anthony; and they hired him. Soon afterwards, Anthony had money saved on a used car. Anthony bought him a used car; and the next day, started driving to school, while working in the afternoon.

Anthony grew to be dedicated to his job and school. He loved working at Red Lobster. Cleaning tables suited his skills because he was quick and athletic. Anthony enjoyed meeting new customers coming into the business. During one point, there was a Caucasian family at a table. Anthony, who was African American was cleaning the table next to them. A Caucasian girl, who was part of the family, tap him on the back. The girl's name was Monica.

Monica replied, "I know you! You go to the Vocational class at my school".

Anthony replied, "You are correct, how are you doing?"

Monica replied, "Just fine, as yourself. If you don't care about me asking, what do you think about white girls?"

Anthony replied, "Never cared to think about them".

Monica replied, "How do you get to work?"

Anthony replied, "In my car."

Monica replied, "I am going to be looking for you in school. I need a boyfriend with transportation".

Anthony figured; she was trying to be nice and flirtish, by giving him a little small talk. The next day, Anthony arrived at his school and parked in the student parking lot. Monica approached Anthony and said hello. Anthony greeted back with a hello.

Monica replied, "Have you ever dated a white girl?"

Anthony replied, "What kind of question is this? Does it look as if I had dated a white girl before? "

Monica replied, "Well, this is going to be interesting. My daddy doesn't like race mixing. I love to make my parents upset. How about we go for a ride and get high?"

Anthony replied, "I don't get high. Besides, I have to go to work after school".

Monica replied, "I want to get high so bad and have sex".

Anthony replied, "I wish, you good luck; you shouldn't have a problem finding somebody".

Monica replied, "You have a car; and I have money. I am not going to make you late for work. We can skip school and get high; until it is time for you to go to work".

Anthony at first, thought maybe she is trying to trick him and use him for his transportation. Why would a white girl want a black guy? Then, he thought this is what is going on in school now all over the country. Interracial dating is what school children want to do now. Anthony never thought about the topic before. He had a few school mates dating outside their race. As far as Anthony was concern, he had no hard feelings against it. Anthony would date any race, as long the girl liked him and treated him with respect. He just loved all girls in general.

Anthony replied, "Okay, we can hang out. Just don't get me in trouble".

Monica replied, "Fine, I want get you in trouble. Do you know anybody which sell drugs?"

Anthony replied, "No, I do not take drugs. I am mostly an alcohol drinker".

Monica replied, “Please, allow me to make a phone call. I bet; somebody has drugs right here in school”.

Monica made a phone call using the school pay phone. In about fifteen minutes, a white guy met her by the school restrooms and sold her drugs. Anthony watched, what was going on and could not believe his eyes, Monica was making a drug deal openly in the school hallway without any protest. Anthony wondered; how often a drug deal occurred in the school hallway.

Anthony replied, “It is this easy, all the time to buy drugs in school”.

Monica replied, “Stick with me; and I can show you a lot of stuff. Now, where can we hang out and relax?”

Anthony replied, “Well, no one is at my house during the day because my mom works during the day”.

Monica replied, “Well, it is official. We are going to your house. Then, we can get high and make out”.

Anthony replied, “Sure, we can do this. Just don’t make me late for work.

Anthony figured; this girl is not going to have risky sex with him. Besides, why is she cutting school and getting high? Monica appeared to be smart; and she had plenty of money. At the restaurant, her family acted as if they cared about her. Therefore, why would she want to make her parents upset? There were so many unanswered questions. Maybe this was a trick; and Monica had a weapon. Monica could be planning on robbing him or something. Anthony was really confused.

When Monica and Anthony arrived at Anthony’s house, Anthony could tell Monica was impressed with the basement. Anthony’s mom had a bar with different types of liquor underneath; and Monica loved looking at the colors and shapes of the liquor bottles. Monica acknowledges, her dad had a bar in his house; and she did the same thing at her home also. While Monica was observing the area, she proceeded to roll a marijuana cigarette. Anthony made him an alcoholic drink. After Monica smoked, she began to rest on the floor.

Monica replied, "Anthony have you ever had sex before?"

Anthony replied, "Why, you asked this?"

Monica replied, "Because you act as a virgin".

Anthony replied, "No, I do not. I am just worried about becoming late for work".

Monica replied, "Hey, I was wanting to have sex. Although, I am not in the mode to be training a virgin".

Anthony thought; something must be wrong with Monica. Monica continually was talking sarcastically about getting high, having sex and other stuff. She mentioned cutting somebody up, if they disappointed her while making love. She talked about making love all night and having sex every day.

Anthony replied, "Monica, I think you are cool but; I am not going to have sex with you. You are far too crazy for me. We can go out together but; friends are all we are going to be and that is the end".

Monica replied, "You are right. I was going to do something freaky to you but, I can tell you are a virgin".

Anthony figured; he would agree with anything Monica said to keep the peace. He did not want anything from Monica because he thought Monica would cause to much trouble. Besides, Monica would not get alone with family or friends he had because of her mood swings. Interracial dating was common in schools, but Anthony did not know how well it was accepted in his family. Anthony believed; Monica had a hidden problem. Maybe her parents were abusing her, and she had been traumatized. Anthony returned Monica back to school and never spent time with her again.

One day, Anthony decided to wash his car in the driveway at his home. School had closed for the day and Anthony did not have to go to work. A school bus had arrived in front of Anthony's house and a girl name Sherri was driving. Anthony had viewed Sherri once a long distance away. He never observed Sherri close until that moment. Simultaneously, Anthony fell in LOVE (Lust on Visual Evidence). Alisa and Julie departed the bus and walked to his vehicle. Alisa and Julie, both gave him a nice compliment on how he was washing his car.

Julie replied, "About time I catch up with you. I have been looking for you".

Anthony replied, "Right, good to see you too Julie".

Alisa replied, "The school year is about to end, are you going to the prom? I know, Julie would be glad to go with you".

Julie replied, "Yes, I sure would".

Anthony replied, "I think I am going to wait until I get in my senior year which is next year.".

Alisa replied, "Anthony are you dating because Julie is looking for a boyfriend?"

Anthony replied, "I don't know".

Julie replied, "You don't know".

Anthony replied, "No, Alisa can I talk to you in private".

Alisa replied, "Sure, what's up?"

Anthony replied, "Alisa, can you fix me up with Sherri?"

Alisa replied, "Sherri the bus driver".

Anthony replied, "Yes!"

Alisa replied, "I probable could, but there is only one problem".

Anthony replied, "What is that?"

Alisa replied, "My friend Julie will kill me. Anthony, you know Julie has a crush on you. Sherri is going through a bad break up with her ex-boyfriend. She had an abortion and her parents prohibit her from dating anytime soon".

Anthony replied, "My luck is bad. Well, tell her I am available if she is looking for a date. We don't have to be serious; I would consider becoming her prom date if she wants to go this year".

Alisa replied, "Okay, what about Julie? Will you consider going on a date with Julie".

Anthony replied, "I don't think so. Tell her we can be friends".

When the school year ended, Anthony was seventeen years old. Anthony thought he would have made some progress with dating Sherri by now. It was strange because Sherri stayed right around the corner from Anthony, but he could not get close enough to meet Sherri. Then, he overheard his school needs additional bus drivers. Sherri was a bus driver's trainer for his school. Anthony figured this was his opportunity to meet Sherri. He signed the list at school to attend bus driver's training.

The first day of the bus driver's training, the principal of the school gave the trainees an orientation and introduced everyone in the class to Sherri. Anthony personally walked up to Sherri and notified her, he heard so much about her. Sherri looked so surprise.

Sherri replied, "I think I know you from somewhere, but where? Okay, I remember you are Alisa friend".

Anthony replied, "Right, I am glad you are my trainer".

Sherri replied, "Why?"

Anthony replied, "I don't know".

Sherri replied, "Alisa said, you have a crush on me."

Anthony replied, "Yes, a little bit".

Sherri replied, "I don't care if you do have a crush on me. I am not going to let you pass that easy. You are going to have to earn your bus driver's license just like I did".

Anthony replied, "Sure, I understand".

Sherri replied, "Do you want to earn you bus driver's license or not? I don't play around with my training time".

Anthony replied, "Yes, I do".

When training started, Anthony had such a hard time learning, he quit the next day. Sherri informed him; he didn't want to learn anyway. Anthony figured; he would never get to know Sherri since he flunked the driver's training. After that, he stops pursuing Sherri for a while. Alisa comes to Anthony house to talk to him.

Alisa replied, "Anthony, what was you thinking about?" I could have told you not to mess with Sherri while she is training drivers. Sherri takes her job very serious".

Anthony replied, "I notice that know".

Alisa replied, "Now, Anthony are you ready to date my friend Julie. You know what you need to do, date someone who cares about you. This is your senior year coming up and you don't need to be lonely. Please date my friend Julie, because she likes you a lot".

Anthony replied, "Alright, I will do it".

One Saturday afternoon, on a pretty day, Anthony was outside watering flowers and Julie was walking up the street. Julie located Anthony in the yard and she stopped to ask could she talk to him. Anthony informed her, sure, we can talk.

Julie replied, "Why don't you like me?"

Anthony replied, "I like you Julie, but as a friend because I really don't know you that well".

Julie replied, "Okay, I am going to visit you all I can until you get to know me".

Julie visited Anthony just about every day in his senior year in school. Alisa noticed Julie was spending a lot of time over Anthony house. Julie was spending more time with Anthony than spending time with Alisa. Alisa became concerned, and she visited Anthony to talk to him.

Alisa replied, "I notice about every day, Julie stops and visits you. Julie and you are becoming close. I have observed the both of you kissing each other in the yard. So, tell me what is really going on?"

Anthony replied, "Nothing, except we are just friends".

Alisa replied, "That is not what Julie is telling me".

Anthony replied, "You know, Julie has a big imagination".

Alisa replied, "I have to inform you, if you hurt my friend, I am going to hurt you".

Anthony replied, "Don't worry, I am not going to hurt Julie".

Alisa replied, "If you do, somebody is going to pay".

DEE JACKSON observed Julie and Anthony kissing in her driveway. After Julie departed, she called Anthony into the house.

DEE JACKSON replied, "I am glad you found a girlfriend, someone who is nice and smart but, I need you to concentrate on your life. Anthony, you are going to have to decide on either college or a career job but either way, you are moving out after you graduate from high school. I cannot have a grown man as a son, living in my house".

Anthony replied, "Okay, I will think about it".

One day Anthony was driving to school, he noticed a bus broke down. A tow truck driver was hooking the bus to his tow truck and Anthony heard someone shouting, wait! Anthony could not believe his eyes, it was Sherri. Sherri opened Anthony car door and sat inside the car on the passenger seat.

Sherri replied, “Hello stranger, you did not see or hear me shouting”.

Anthony replied, “Yes, I saw you and I was not about to leave until you showed up at my car”.

Sherri replied, “It is bad when you are a bus driver and the bus break down. It takes forever for someone to pick you up. If I had a boyfriend, it would not be a problem. I would call my boyfriend and he would solve my problems”.

Anthony replied, “I guess”.

Sherri replied, “So, who is the lucky girl that is your girlfriend?”

Anthony replied, “I don’t have a girlfriend”.

Sherri replied, “You are not telling me a lie or you?”

Anthony replied, “You think I would lie to you. No way”.

Sherri replied, “Okay, here is my phone number, wait for me after school and give me a ride home.

Anthony replied, “Okay”.

Anthony could not believe it. He dropped Sherri off at school and could not wait until school ended so he could pick Sherri back up and take her home. School ended, and Anthony waited for Sherri in the student parking lot. Sherri located Anthony in the parking lot and began to smile.

Sherri replied, “I am so glad to see you, I wanted to have a long talk with you. To tell you the truth, I had a crush on you, ever since you took that bus driver’s class. Anthony, that took a lot of courage. I was impressed with you back then, but I could not express it because I am a Jehovah witness and my parents did not want me to date”.

Anthony replied, “I understand your situation”.

Sherri replied, “I am a senior in school and parents have to understand, we have to live our lives. If Anthony, you want to be my boyfriend, I just want you to do a couple of things”.

Anthony replied, “What is that”.

Sherri replied, “We must see each other secretly. My parents must not find out about you until we graduate from high school. I do not want my parents to find out I am dating”.

Anthony replied, “That is fine with me”.

Anthony began to think, Alisa told him, Sherri dated a guy and she had an abortion. So, why would Sherri’s parents care if she be seen with another guy. Anthony figured as long he did not get her pregnant, he should be in good standings forever with her parents. Anthony got ready to park his car in his driveway at home. Sherri notified him to take her home first, because she had something to do and her parents were at work.

Anthony replied, “Sherri are you sure you want to go home”.

Sherri replied, “Yes, wait for me in my driveway”.

Anthony replied, “Well, while I wait, can I get a glass of water?”

Sherri replied, “Yes, when I get in the house, I will meet you at the back door”.

Anthony and Sherri arrived at Sherri’s house and Anthony parked in front of the house. Sherri departed the car and entered her house through the front door. Anthony exited his car and walked to the back door of Sherri’s house. Right about the same time, another car pulled up in Sherri’s driveway. It was Sherri’s parents.

Sherri’s father replied, “I am done saying that girl about having boys in the house. This is the final straw”.

CHAPTER EIGHT

# LIFE DECISION

Sherri's parents got out their vehicle and walked to the front door. Anthony politely listens to Sherri's parents go inside the house, then he ran back to his car. He engaged his car into drive and drove off. Anthony thought, that was a close call. Sherri almost got him in trouble. What in the world, was on her mind? The next day, Sherri's parents drove her to school. Sherri located Anthony in the school lobby area and addressed him upset.

Sherri replied, "Anthony, you got me in big trouble. Now, I am grounded until further notice. I might go out again until prom night. Then, again I might still be grounded".

Anthony replied, "I apologize for the inconvenience".

That was the end of Anthony relationship with Sherri. Anthony was planning to go to the prom with Sherri, but his plans was ruined. In returned, Anthony ended up skipping the prom and hanging out with his guy friends on prom night. Anthony's friends influence him to carpool to the movies and boycott the prom. They arrived in Greensboro, NC, at some XXX movie theater, where he got sick because he observed a freaky sex act on the movie screen. The next day Anthony had a hangover and DEE JACKSON had a long mother to son talk with Anthony.

DEE JACKSON replied, "Anthony you are my son so, I am obligated to tell you because it appears you need advising. The birds and the bees, I cannot teach you because you are seventeen and going on eighteen. But what I can tell you is to find a soul mate. Your soul mate must be someone you deeply care about and feels the same way about you. Also, it would be good if she works and gives respect for herself and others. In return, that means Julie should not be kissing you in the front yard or outside in public. Public display of affection between the both of you in my front yard or anywhere else, where someone is watching is a disrespect to me, her, you and to someone else maybe because you all are not married".

Anthony replied, "Oh, I am sorry about that".

DEE JACKSON replied, "Have you made a decision on what you are going to do after high school".

Anthony replied, "I am joining the Army, like my daddy joined the Air Force and my brother joined the Navy".

DEE JACKSON replied, "You are going to join the military. Well, why not the Air Force like your dad".

Anthony replied, "No, no good because my school only had an Army Recruiter, enlisting students".

Later, Anthony notified his father, he was joining the Army before he graduates from high school. Anthony's brother B.J called home and spoke to him, on the phone.

B.J replied, "Hey little brother, mom tells me you decided to leave home and join the Army".

Anthony replied, "Yes".

B.J replied, "I hope you have good luck. I have decided to only do my time and I am coming back home. So, how is the dating world at home".

Anthony replied, "The same as usual".

B.J replied, "Have you gotten lucky yet? I know you not still a virgin. You might as well sleep with Julie, the girl around the corner".

Anthony replied, "Julie is not my type. I don't feel she is pretty enough".

B.J replied, "Anthony, who cares. The only thing you need, is to have sex before you leave to the military. You do not want to be horny; you need to have a little experience with girls in sex".

Anthony replied, "I just waste time with Julie".

B.J replied, "I know but who else you have available. The only girl I know you socialize with is Alisa and her friend Julie. You need to choose who is your best option".

Anthony replied, "Alisa is more pretty but she is a tom boy".

B.J replied, "Your choices are limited, and Julie wants you anyway. You need to give in to Julie, she might make a man out of you".

So, Anthony meditated what his brother said and the next day Julie visited Anthony at his house. Anthony informs to Julie, after he graduates from high school, he is leaving for the military. Julie is extremely upset and sheds a tear. Anthony attempts to comfort her by hugging her tight. DEE JACKSON looks out the window and waves her index finger representing no physical affection. Anthony moves Julie away from DEE JACKSON sights and stops hugging Julie.

Anthony replied, "Julie you do not have to worry, I probably will be away about six months before I complete my job training. Then, I will be home temporary to visit.

Julie replied, "But, graduation is almost here, and we have maybe two months to spend time with each other".

Anthony replied, “Yes, I know. We just have to make the most of it”.

Julie replied, “Anthony, you probably will go away and find another girl”.

Anthony replied, “I don’t think so. They might not even have girls, where I am going”.

Julie replied, “I want to give you something to remember me. This way you want be looking at other girls. I want to make love to you and I want you to promise while you are gone you will try to be faithful to me. I promise, while you are away, I will be faithful to you”.

Anthony replied, “Julie, you do not have to prove anything to me”.

Julie replied, “No, I want to do this”

Anthony replied, “Okay Julie, if you really want to make love, we can spend some time alone at my house when my mom is at work after school”.

The next day, Alisa visits Anthony. Alisa informed Anthony, Julie told her, Anthony is joining the military and they were going to get intimate before Anthony decides to leave for good.

Alisa replied, “What is this, I hear you are about to make an important move?

Anthony replied, "Yes, at first I wasn’t sure but, I thought, I am a senior in high school about to graduate. It is time, I must decide with my life. So, I agreed to volunteer”.

Alisa replied, “So, you volunteered to have sex with my girlfriend Julie”.

Anthony replied, “I am not talking about Julie”.

Alisa replied, “I am talking about Julie”.

Anthony replied, "Oh, okay she told you our plans”.

Alisa replied, "Yes, Julie tells me everything. When you finish having sex with my friend, what are going to do then".

Anthony replied, "Oh, she did not tell you my plans afterwards".

Alisa replied, "Tell me what".

Anthony replied, "I am joining the Army".

Alisa replied, "The Army!  Anthony, you done lost your mind. I know you are trying to commit suicide now".

Anthony replied, "No Alisa, it is called becoming a man and serving my country".

Alisa replied, "So, you are doing all this to become a man".

Anthony replied, "No, I need a change of life. My mother told me; I must move out after high school.

Alisa replied, "I am going to community college and get a job. Why don't you join me? We can help each other out in school".

Anthony replied, "I wish you had suggested that idea, before I signed my name on the enlistment contract".

Alisa replied, "Julie and you have been hanging so much together. I haven't had the time to talk to you alone. You do not have to do this, if you don't want too. There is time still left".

Anthony replied, "I told my mother already. My plans are set".

Alisa replied, "This is your life, Anthony. Go to college with me and forget about the military and Julie. If you don't like Julie as your girlfriend, do not have sex with her. Anthony, you are a good-looking guy, allow Julie to find a man who really likes her".

Anthony was shocked to hear Alisa make remarks like that. He could not remember Alisa saying anything about him as nice. Anthony felt sad and started to regret he made plans so quickly. Anthony began to second guess how he felt about Alisa. Alisa was not a bad looking girl. She was no beauty model, but her wisdom made up for her looks and personality. If Anthony had to choose between Alisa and Julie, Alisa would win every time. But there were only few times where Alisa and Anthony made a love connection. Anthony wishes now, he had paid more attention to Alisa.

A week had past, and the phone rang. Anthony picks up the receiver on the phone and it was Julie. Julie had informed Anthony, Alisa and she were no longer friends anymore. Alisa told Julia to break up with Anthony because they were not compatible and distance relationships are too hard on young people unless they really love each other. Julie was all tears. Julia could not believe; Alisa would advise her to do that. Julie told Anthony; he is the only person she socialized with now.

Anthony replied, "I am sorry about the situation".

Julie replied, "Anthony are you alone and is your mother at work now?"

Anthony replied, "Yes".

Julie replied, "Would you like for me to visit you now, where we can have some time alone to make love".

Anthony replied, "Sure!"

Julie walked over to Anthony's house. Anthony allowed Julie to enter the house and into his bedroom. Julie and Anthony both begin to undress slowly in front of each other and Julie slid underneath the bed covers. Anthony followed by sliding underneath the covers on the other side. Julie grabs his hand to direct him to lay on top of her. Anthony laid on top of her and kisses her forehead. Anthony thinks how proud his brother would be if he only knew this was happening. Then, he thinks about his mother advise. DEE JACKSON told him he needs a girlfriend who cares about him and herself and he should also do the same for her. Also, Alisa informed him, if you do not want Alisa as a girlfriend do not have sex with her.

Anthony began to feel Julie's body; how warm and soft it was from her face down to her toes. He positions his hips into her private area. Anthony slowly grinds with his hips and he notice how moist she was becoming. He did not penetrate with his private at no times, he just observed the expressions on her face after she closed her eyes. Julie began to make noises of enjoyment. Anthony rub Julie thighs up and down simultaneously as if he was a machine.

Julie replied, "Please Anthony do not stop, just don't get me pregnant".

Anthony replied, "Right, I cannot do that".

Anthony laid next to Julie for a little while and then he got up and put his clothes on. Julie got up and did the same. They both entered the living room and watch T.V for a few minutes. Anthony informed Julie; she needs to be leaving before his mother come in from work.

Julie replied, "I had fun, can I come visit you tomorrow and we can do this again".

Anthony replied, "The next time, we have to meet somewhere else because I do not feel comfortable in my mom house".

Julie replied, "I feel so happy now. I will call you later".

After Julie left, Anthony figured he must be dumb. Anthony thought, he almost jeopardized his life. He could had gotten Julie pregnant and his life would have been over. Anthony was glad he didn't go all the way with Julie. Julie claimed she was satisfied and that was good enough for him. Anthony wondered should he feel different towards Julie now since they were interment. Not really, he still felt like he wished he had paid more attention to Alisa. Anthony becoming interment with Julie gave him an appetite for sex. He was on the edge mentally to be with someone he thought was worthy, and he thought was fine.

The sensation of being next to a nude body was overwhelming. Anthony did not want to be with Julie anymore. Julie was nice, but he wanted something better. Anthony body was craving for sex. He thought okay, I am turning eighteen soon and maybe his body is going through changes.

CHAPTER NINE

# JOINING THE ARMY

The day of Anthony's eighteen birthday his brother came home from the Navy. B.J asked what he wanted for his birthday. Anthony requested from his brother to buy him a bottle of liquor. He had no plans but to get drunk and relax at home. Julie called Anthony to spend time with him, but he denied the option. Then, Alisa showed up later to wish Anthony happy birthday.

Alisa replied, "Anthony are you still going into the military after high school graduation".

Anthony replied, "Yes, I think this is the right thing to do".

Alisa replied, "I just want to wish you good luck and spend some time with you on your birthday".

Anthony replied, "Great, we will have a seat in the basement, relax and enjoy some time".

Alisa replied, "What are you drinking?"

Anthony replied, "My brother bought me some liquor for my birthday. Please be my guest and have a drink with me".

Anthony planned to get Alisa drunk for his enjoyment. Alisa watched Anthony drink shots after shots as she turned down request for her to drink. Anthony gets drunk and pass out on the floor. B.J politely escorts Alisa to the exit door, so she could go home. Anthony dreams of having sex with Alisa in the basement. The next morning, he wakes up on the basement floor hugging a pillow talking about, I love you, Alisa. Anthony then vomits on the floor and B.J comes to his assistance. He looks around for Alisa and ask B.J, didn't Alisa spend the night with him down in the basement. B.J notifies him, only in your dreams. I let Alisa out the back door while you were asleep on the floor. Anthony was so disappointed.

Anthony replied, "Well, at least I made out with Julie before I depart".

B.J replied, "Oh, you did. No wonder you look different and acting all cocky. Now, you are trying to seduce Alisa and get her drunk on your birthday. That was wishful thinking, but you should have been doing something like that a long time ago. You have waited too late to sleep with Alisa. When were you going to tell me about Julie? Julie, she is going to tell Alisa, you slept with her. Then, you can forget about having anything to do with Alisa".

Anthony replied, "Yes, I know. Therefore, I wanted to give a finale try".

B.J replied, "Poor little brother, your chances for love is the same for Alisa, which is zero. I guess Julie will be waiting for you but, you don't even want Julie".

Then B.J starts laughing but, Anthony was not laughing. Anthony felt depressed deep down inside. Anthony did not like his brother making fun of his love life. B. J's sarcasm was creating doubt in Anthony; he will never find the right girl for himself. It appeared to Anthony, B.J was right after all. B.J had been dating his soul mate since he graduate from high school. Anthony wondered how B.J got so lucky and he couldn't. He prayed; the military had better opportunities for finding love.

Anthony's graduation ceremony was a happy event. All Anthony's close family attended the event. Julie showed up at his house after the graduation was over. Julie gave him, her departure farewell speech. She reiterated for Anthony to stay safe and write whenever possible. Alisa was graduation from school also, and she gave her goodbyes. She informed him; it is still not too late for him to change his mind about the military.

The next day, the Army Recruiter arrived at Anthony's house during the morning. Then suddenly, Anthony departed to the Army Recruiting Station in Charlotte, NC. Anthony traveled in the Recruiter van, while the Recruiter informed him about the Army. It was four other recruits in the van, which was three guys and one female. Anthony was nervous and began to have anxiety.

Then, there was rigorous test conducted but, he was able to pass satisfactory. The rest of the recruits who passed, spent a night at the station including Anthony. Everyone was shipped to their designated training base due to their job choice. Anthony was forwarded to Ft Sill, OK, where he spent four long months of basic training. At this place, he trained to be physically and mentally prepared for combat service. Anthony's main occupation in the military was administrative clerk.

The Army Recruiter showed him a video clip of his duties and he notice the training was for coed personnel. That meant males and females were combine for training purposes. But before he reached that stage of training, he first had to complete basic training and then, he was sent to Ft Jackson for occupation school or AIT. While he was at Ft Sill, he wondered was there a mistake because no women were training on the base. Anthony realized; it was an all-artillery outfits unit only. Then, when he completed training at Ft Sill, OK and departed to Ft Jackson, SC, he felt more comfortable because there were women training in the area. It began to appear more civilized as on the video clip.

Anthony encountered the most attractive women in the Army at Ft Jackson, SC. There were women from all fifty states in the United States, consisting of Reserves, National Guard, and Regular Army. Anthony became pleased with the variety of people he observed on the base. He wished society in his neighborhood reflected the culture which the military base showed. Anthony was confident, he picked the best occupation for his personality and in the process, maybe he could meet a nice girl.

The job training was fun and ideal to what Anthony wanted to learn. Anthony was never a person who enjoyed manual labor on the outside. The Army taught him Inter Office skills and how to manage office procedures. This made Anthony very confident in business and in the office area. While Anthony was taking a break from training in the office, he decided to snack at the picnic table area outside. Two girls who were snacking at the picnic tables, who appeared to be close to his age, asked him why he was so quiet and anti-social.

Anthony replied, "I didn't know people paid attention to me. I always have been quiet and have had difficult times meeting friends".

One of the two girls name Glory was dark skinned, had long hair and was very outspoken. She was doing most of the talking. The other girl's name Valery was reserved. She had long hair, green eyes and I could not tell what her ethnicity was. Valery was very pretty, interesting looking but aggressive. She was five foot and nine inches tall with light skinned from Los Angeles, CA".

Glory replied, "My name is Glory. I am from St Louis, Mo; and I think you are handsome. Meet me after class, where we can get to know each other in the break area. I am single; and we can do some things after class".

Anthony could not help but notice; Glory friend Valery was licking her lips at him while Glory was talking to him. Later, he heard of Valery was an ex-teenage model for Sears catalog magazine. Valery just stared at him; and he could not resist starring back at her.

Valery replied, "What is your name? Is it Anthony, I think? There is something different about you. I have been observing you; and I noticed you haven't tried to talk to no girls in class or nobody. I can tell, you are quiet. I want you to be my boyfriend. I like a guy, who keeps to himself".

Glory replied, "Valery, don't waste your time. He is a virgin or gay, I can tell. If you are not gay then, I want you to have sex with me at the picnic table. Prove to me, you are not gay or a virgin".

Anthony was shocked and overwhelmed. He could not think of a response fast enough to reply. There were other guys, who were observing what was going on and responded out loud. They shouted, "He must be gay because he is not saying anything or doing anything". Anthony was disappointed in himself because he was slow thinking. Anxiety had control over him once again. One guy name Bobby, who was participating in the crowd, overlooking what was going on became the main instigator. Bobby walked up to Glory.

Bobby replied, "My name is Bobby; and I will be your boyfriend".

Glory replied, "I appreciate the offer but; I was talking to this guy name Anthony.

Bobby replied, "If he doesn't want you then, I do. I would like to be your friend".

Bobby walked over to Anthony. He replied, "You must be gay. How can you turn down an invitation to be with a pretty girl?" Anthony did not say anything. He shook his head and walked away. The next day, Anthony met Glory and Valery in training. Glory informed Anthony, she would give him one more chance to meet her after hours at the picnic table. Anthony informed Glory; he doesn't want any problems. He only wants to finish AIT training without any worries.

Valery replied, "I apologized for my friend. She is ghetto. We can be friends and meet at the bowling alley".

Anthony replied, "Okay but; I don't want no trouble".

When Anthony arrived at the bowling alley, Valery was sitting at the table alone. Then, Anthony surveyed the bowling alley and approached the table where Valery was sitting. Soon as Anthony began to sit down, Bobby, Glory and their associates approach the table.

Bobby replied, "Valery, what are you doing with this fag".

Valery replied, "Leave Anthony alone, he is not gay. Anthony is going to be my boyfriend".

Glory replied, "Hey Valery, Bobby has a friend. He wants to introduce you to him".

Valery replied, "Glory, no offense. I do not want to meet nobody else. Anthony, can we please go somewhere else".

Anthony replied, "No problem!"

Valery and Anthony walked outside to stop a cab passing by. The cab stopped and both Valery and Anthony get inside. Valery puts her hand on Anthony crotch and licks him in the ear. Anthony cannot believe what is happening. Valery was a good-looking half-breed model from Los Angeles. Anthony figured; he was below her standards because he was from a small town.

Valery replied, "It is close for us to graduate from military occupation school. Then, we will separate. Every student in school is going to go out on dates and celebrate their diplomas. They will be staying in motels and eating at fancy restaurants. I am going to stay at the Holiday Inn Motel, where they have a luxury nightclub and bar. I can make reservations for you and me to receive a discount packet".

Anthony thought; he only known Valery for a short period. Military Occupation training last only four weeks so, it would be a month; they would have known each other. Although, this could be a chance of a lifetime. To be in a nice motel with a beautiful, attractive young girl was a dream of a lifetime. What if it be just a month's time to have known somebody. Anthony had to accept this invitation. Anthony was only eighteen; and she was the same age also.

Anthony replied, "Yes, I will definitely be there at the motel, come check in time".

Valery replied, "Great, I am going to make the reservations. Cab driver take us back to our barracks!"

Prior to graduation, Anthony notified his parents. He was graduation at Ft Jackson, SC. Anthony's parents notified him; they were driving to Anthony graduation ceremony in South Carolina to watch him March in an auditorium. Anthony informed his parents the time and location. His parents notified him; his brother will attend also. He made a note to advise them on room reservations and tour plans of the base on the barracks telephone.

Anthony replied, "Hello B.J, I am calling you on the phone to update you about plans while at Ft Jackson. I have a girlfriend. I want you to meet her. Her name is Valery; and she is the prettiest girl, I have ever dated. For some unknown reason, she likes me; and I do not know why".

B.J replied, "Oh really, I have to see her then. Your mother will be surprised".

Anthony replied, “Yes, she will. In addition, I will return home with you all. I have thirty days leave before I report overseas”.

B.J replied, “Report overseas and to what country!”

Anthony replied, “They tell me South Korea”.

B.J replied, “Wow! Please notify your mother”.

When the day of graduation arrived, all the graduating students was excited. This was the day, a lot of students waited for patiently. They dream about this moment, mostly their entire lives. Some students wanted to be a Military service person since they were young. Other students had been away from home for six months or more. Anthony was one, who was away for six months without seeing home. He was anxious to see his parents and brother from North Carolina, while taking a break from military training. Once Anthony family arrived at Ft Jackson, SC, he was able to spend a little time with them.

Anthony directed his family on a tour guide of the military base. Then, the graduation ceremony started. The graduation ceremony was long but; it was worth Anthony family making the long travel. After the graduation, Anthony introduced Valery to his family; and Valery introduced her family to Anthony. Everyone was happy and having a good time. Anthony was unsure if Valery was going to continue with her plans to stay in a motel. He figured; while Valery’s family was here, she might want to return to her home early. After the closing moments of graduation, Valery made it known; she wanted to spend time with Anthony at the Holiday Inn Motel. Valery’s family complied because she informed them ahead of time; and they were tired.

Valery’s parents told her they probably will never make a trip like this again so; enjoy herself because this will be the only time. Anthony's parents told him to enjoy his self also because he deserved it.

B.J replied, "Anthony, Valery is a pretty enough girl. I hope you can handle everything she is capable of bringing.".

After everyone departed the graduation ceremony, Anthony directed his family to their motel rooms. The motel where Anthony's family had reservations was a block away from where Valery was staying. It was great because Anthony could drive his mom's vehicle and arrive at the Holiday Inn within five minutes away. When the night came, Anthony's brother and he began to change into their party clothes.

B.J replied, "Anthony are you sure, you want to drive".

Anthony replied, "Sure, I am fine".

B.J replied, "Okay! Now, if you need back up, let me know".

Anthony replied, "Well brother, I do have a favor. Valery has a room to herself at the Holiday Inn. I believe, she is going to want me to stay all night with her. If possible, will you take mom's car and return it back to her tonight. Then, pick me up in the morning".

B.J replied, "You are trying to make one more try for romance; I hear you!"

Anthony replied, "I guess, I am".

B.J replied, "You lucky dog. Give me the word; and I see you in the morning".

When Anthony and B.J arrived at the Holiday Inn, a party was starting in the Motel club area. Both Anthony and B.J had already had a drink or two before they departed. They found a table fast because they were early. Anthony noticed; a lot of people were there from the graduation. B.J inquired to him; this must be the place for the official after party from the graduation because this place is getting packed. They both observed women walking in and out; and B.J commented on how beautiful the women were at the party.

B.J replied, "Anthony, if you don't mind, I might pay for a room at this motel too. I think, I am in heaven".

Anthony replied, "I think, you are right. This is God's gift to man, right here".

Then, Valery walks in. She was stunning, wearing a low-cut blouse with tight black slacks and black high heel shoes. Anthony was informed by B.J again; how lucky he was. Valery glanced at the crowd of people and then, she noticed Anthony. She politely walked up to him and then, greeted B.J.

Valery replied, "Hello, you all made it. You look wonderful Anthony; please let's dance".

Anthony replied, "Sure, I have been waiting for this".

B.J sat at the table and watched Valery and Anthony dance for half a minute. The disc jockey played a new song; and Anthony worst nightmare happen. This gigantic man escorted by Valery's friend Glory and her boyfriend Bobby, tap Anthony on the shoulder.

The gigantic man replied, "Excuse me but; little man this is my girlfriend. I want to dance with her now".

B.J looked at Anthony. Valery was shocked. Anthony started wondering; why do unsuspecting things happens to him. At first, Anthony figured; I need to just turn around and walk the other way but; his anxiety took over.

Anthony replied, "Look dude, I know this girl; and we have been dating since she has been in South Carolina".

Anthony was lucky; B.J thought quickly and told everybody, his brother was drunk; and he doesn't know no better. B.J informed Valery to go ahead and dance with the other gentleman. He will escort Anthony to his car.

B.J replied, “Valery, you are so pretty; and my brother thinks, he can fight anybody for your love. Do not worry people, I am going to take him home. He will not bother you anymore”. Then, he informed Anthony; it was time for him to go home now.

Anthony replied, “What? Oh yes, you are very much correct brother. I don’t know what, I was doing. Get me out of here”.

B.J and Anthony both returned to their mother’s car.

B.J replied, “Wow, this was a close one. What came over you little brother?”

Anthony replied, “I don’t know. My anxiety took control over me. I wanted Valery so bad. Thank goodness, I finally came to my senses”.

B.J replied, “Thank God because I thought, I was about to lose a brother”.

Anthony replied, “Thanks for the rescue”.

After that incident, Anthony became cautious of extremely attractive girls. B.J informed him; he needs to be taught, if a girl is going to jeopardize his safety, she is not worthy of his time. Before you date a woman, try to judge her personality; and be very careful. Anthony had informed his family; Valery was from Los Angeles. B.J informed him; girls who are raised in big cities are always attracting bad company; or they are bad company. Always be careful of extremely attractive women.

Anthony replied, “B.J, you are so correct. I was just praying; this girl was the one for me”.

B.J replied, “If you see a woman flirting with you and she show real interest, be careful and observe for any bad behavior.

When Anthony returned home, he received paperwork for his assignment to active duty in Korea. Somehow, Julie found out he was at home. Then, Julie visited Anthony.

Julie replied, "I wrote you letters but; there was no reply".

Anthony replied, "I received the letters but; the military training had me too busy to respond. Now, I am going to my regular duty. I will have no time to write back".

Julie replied, "Anthony, you better write me back".

Although, Anthony had no intentions of having a committed relationship with Julie anymore. It was nice to receive love letters from her. Dee Jackson informed Anthony numerous of times about misleading Julie. Dee Jackson made it clear; she would rather see me with Julie than for me to date a foreigner overseas.

Dee Jackson replied, "When, you get to Korea; I understand, you might be lonely. Whomever, you be with to pass time away. Please, leave it there in Korea. I do not want a slant eyed in my family".

Anthony realized; there was no end to the advice his family had to give in any situation. After a month had passed, Anthony took a plane from his hometown to Korea, where his duty station was located. Anthony tried to remember all the advice he had been given, especially from his brother. His brother advice appeared to be the most helpful. Anthony had to transfer planes in St Louis before going to Korea. He was waiting in the lobby, while sitting in the chair; and this beautiful girl approached him. She introduced herself as Olivia.

Olivia replied, "I noticed, you are in the military by your outfit. I wondered, if you could please buy me a drink at the bar. I am short on change. I was wondering, if you could be helpful; and do me a favor".

Anthony replied, "I guess, if I buy you one drink, it wouldn't' t hurt none".

Anthony thought about what his brother said about pretty girls. He figured, he just got paid; and he had money to spare.

He bought the girl a drink, thinking it wouldn't hurt none. Anthony walked up to the bar and buys a coke with Jack Daniels liquor and gives it to Olivia. Olivia turns around and hands the drink to another guy. Anthony could not believe; she did that. Now, Anthony knows for a fact B.J was right; pretty girls are nothing but trouble.

As Anthony continued to travel on the next plane to Korea, he wonders will everything be okay in the military. Anthony also wonders will Korea have nice looking women or will they have women which gets you in trouble. The intention is to find a girl, he has something in common with and hopeful have a good time while he is over in Korea. Anthony is not trying to get hustled. He doesn't care how pretty the girls appear to be now because he is not trying to be fooled by looks. This kind of girl will just have to find another guy to trick.

When Anthony touched down in Korea, there was an escort who pick him up from the airport and drop him off at his barracks. Anthony observed his company area and noticed; the military base specialized in infantry. Most infantry units consisted of male personnel only. The base Anthony was assigned to had ninety percent males, which left only ten percent females. Anthony's company had mostly all the females assigned to his unit. Anthony's unit and another one was the only coed unit out of twenty units on base.

The first day of work, Anthony's supervisor name Staff Sergeant Kapp greeted him and gave everyone who was new an orientation.

Staff Sergeant Kapp replied, "I am here to give you information about Korea. This place is not the best place but; you are only here for a year. To make the best out of your assignment, go sightseeing, take up a hobby, or attend college classes on base. If you feel lonely or depressed, talk to me and talk to an Army counselor because we have plenty of counselors here to help. In addition, before you are thinking about committing suicide, talk to your family members and talk to me because we have help for that too".

Staff Sergeant Kapp was an experience military employee who knew the ways to survive at the military station in Korea. He was a regular expert but; he was stubborn in his own ways. Staff Sergeant Kapp believed; if it wasn't done his way you had to hit the highway because nobody was going to change him. Anthony was in Korea about a week; when his supervisor told him to go out, leave the barracks and have some fun. Anthony stayed to himself so; his supervisor introduced Anthony to a new soldier named Brooklyn.

Staff Sergeant Kapp replied, "Private Anthony, I want you to meet Private Brooklyn, who is a new employee as yourself. I would like you all to work close together; and help each other out. Private Brooklyn and you are the same age or have the same background so; if possible, please stay together".

Anthony replied, "Yes, Staff Sergeant Kapp. I will try to do that".

Anthony thought at first, this shouldn't be a problem; but later it became a nuisance. Everywhere Private Brooklyn was located, Staff Sergeant Kapp wanted Anthony to keep an eye on her. One day Staff Sergeant Kapp knock on Anthony room door and expected Brooklyn to be in the room. Anthony got tired of Staff Sergeant Kapp asking questions about Brooklyn and commented, do I suppose to be Private Brooklyn's keeper all the time. Anthony assumed because Staff Sergeant Kapp was the supervisor, he shouldn't be the one to keep up with Brooklyn all the time.

Private Brooklyn was a nice attractive female. Anthony thought she was goofy, always late for meetings and had no knowledge of anything important. Anthony also figured; Brooklyn and him, had nothing in common. Staff Sergeant Kapp finally put his foot down and placed Anthony strictly in charge of Private Brooklyn.

Staff Sergeant Kapp replied, "Brooklyn and you, Anthony are battle buddies until further notice with you in charge. This means, you take care of Brooklyn as if your life depends on it".

Private Brooklyn replied, "How come, he is the one in charge? We are the same rank".

Staff Sergeant Kapp replied, "Because I said so".

Once again, Anthony knew, this was going to be a problem because Brooklyn was good looking, single, and there were a lot of lonely man around. Before Anthony knew it, he was Private Brooklyn's personal escort. Then, a guy who has a wife in the United States began to date Brooklyn; and Staff Sergeant Kapp disapproved. Staff Sergeant Kapp told Private Brooklyn not to date him.

Staff Sergeant Kapp replied, "Private Brooklyn, if you want to date someone then, it only can be Private Anthony. Private Anthony is available because he has never been married and has no kids".

Private Brooklyn replied, "I have nothing in common with Private Anthony; and he is too nice. I will think about it".

Later, Anthony barracks had training; and Staff Sergeant Kapp asked about Private Brooklyn. Anthony told him; he had no clue about her where abouts.

Staff Sergeant Kapp replied, "I have never seen a guy in the military who don't care about an attractive female. Anthony, have you tried to get close to Brooklyn? You know, she is pretty and attractive".

Anthony replied, "No, not really".

Staff Sergeant Kapp replied, "What is it, either you are gay; or you too shy".

Anthony replied, "Neither one".

Staff Sergeant Kapp replied, "Well then, you are scared of girls".

Anthony replied, "I am not scared of girls".

Staff Sergeant replied, "I am going to get my best soldier to take you outside the gate and fix you up with a woman downtown. You need a woman because you be scared to talk to Brooklyn. If you turn me down then, I know you are gay. I will tell the entire military base, how you are gay".

Anthony assumed; Staff Sergeant Kapp was serious because he got in contact with his best employee soldier and rush him to meet Anthony. It made Anthony think; Staff Sergeant Kapp would do anything, he felt needed to be done. The soldier escorted Anthony outside the gate. He asked Anthony, what kind of Korean woman he liked: big chested, tall, short or light complexion. It did not matter. To Anthony, it did not matter because he wasn't interested at all.

When the soldier escorted Anthony outside the gate, Anthony started to experience anxiety because he never walked outside the gate. The soldier escorted him to an establishment where there was a bar. Also, the waitresses serving food and drinks. It was fixed up like a family restaurant. The soldier politely spoke to a man in a stern tone, working behind the bar.

The soldier replied, "I need a girl for a short time and make sure she is the best you got".

The soldier gave the man fifty dollars; and the man walked to another room. Then, the soldier had Anthony to walk down a hallway, which lead to a bedroom. The soldier informed Anthony; not to try and go into the bedroom but wait by the bedroom door, until the man and him come down. When

Anthony walked down the hallway, there was a chair posted beside the door. Anthony sat down in the chair and waited. In ten minutes, an attractive Korean lady escorted by the soldier walked by Anthony and entered the bedroom.

The soldier replied, "Wait until I come out; and then you walk in.

After fifteen minutes, the soldier walks out the room while straightening his clothes on his body. The soldier replied, "Anthony, you are next. Hurry up and get in there!" Anthony walks in the room cautiously while his anxiety is going. The woman is laying on the bed, under the covers in the nude. The woman is awake and informs Anthony; get undress and slide in bed.

Anthony replied, "I have something important to say. I never had sex before".

The woman replied, "It's okay and smiled. There is a first time for everything".

The woman stands up and directs Anthony by the bed. She grabs Anthony and forces him to lay on the bed. Then, she rolls Anthony on top of her. The woman politely grabs his bottom and pushes him inside her until Anthony decides to climax. After the sex is finished, Anthony gathers himself and puts his clothes on. Anthony realizes, he is no longer a virgin anymore. He thinks, should I celebrate; but for some reason, he feels dirty. Anthony wished; his first time was not with a prostitute. He wished; it was with somebody, he loved and wanted to be with. The sexual experience made Anthony feel less than a Christian.

Anthony returned to his barracks. He cursed secretly to himself at Staff Sergeant Kapp, the soldier, the prostitute and sex altogether. Then, he thought; what have I done. How could I allow something as this to happen to me? What kind of world am I living in which allow stuff like this to happen? The next day, he did not want to look at Staff Sergeant Kapp. Staff Sergeant Kapp laughed and laughed at Private Anthony. The soldier bragged how he had sex with the prostitute; and Anthony, he hated the world for a while. But the feeling, did not last too long because Staff Sergeant Kapp antagonized Anthony whenever possible.

Staff Sergeant Kapp replied, "I know you would like to date Brooklyn now. You are experience now so; are you ready for Private Brooklyn; or do you need the Korean prostitute again".

Anthony had no love for Staff Sergeant Kapp or his comments. Anthony tried to ignore his supervisor and perform his job well. In the process, Anthony began to hang out at clubs and exercise. On one occasion, Private Brooklyn happen to notice Anthony off duty going to the club. She informed him he had been acting different and looked different.

Private Brooklyn replied, "There is something very different about you".

Anthony replied, "Why; because I am going out and trying to have a good time".

Private Brooklyn replied, "No, it is because you are acting more mature. You are looking different also".

Anthony replied, "I am trying to get in shape and take my mind of a lot of things".

Private Brooklyn replied, "Well, whatever you are doing, keep doing it because you look good".

CHAPTER TEN

# INTRO TO RENA MY WIFE

Private Brooklyn made Anthony very happy. Brooklyn decided to hang out with Anthony to exercise and lose weight. Anthony tried to coach her and help her with push-ups and sit ups. When Brooklyn realized; what Anthony was teaching, it helped her in her exercise. Private Brooklyn turned around and gave Anthony a hug and a kiss. Anthony began to see Brooklyn differently and fell in love with Private Brooklyn. Then, Private Brooklyn's and Private Anthony's duty in Korea was coming to an end. Anthony wondered; why life had to be unfair, just as when Private Brooklyn and he were getting close.

Staff Sergeant Kapp made an announcement to individuals, when they came up for time to leave their duty base. Private Brooklyn leave orders showed for her to be assigned to Ft Polk, LA; and Anthony was on notice for Ft Benning, GA. Anthony could tell Brooklyn was sad about leaving because of her eye contact. Private Brooklyn informed Anthony; she enjoyed her time, especially when it came to the end. She wanted to spend her last days in Korea on a weekend with Anthony together. Then, rumors began to escalate she had a sexual relationship with Staff Sergeant Kapp.

Anthony could not believe the rumors but; it was true. Staff Sergeant Kapp wanted Anthony to keep his eye on Private Brooklyn for himself. There was a rumor which spread; Private Brooklyn was pregnant by Staff Sergeant Kapp. Although later, Anthony found out this was not true. Finally, Anthony decided to skip the weekend with Private Brooklyn and concentrate on his own departure. Anthony used his own private time to pack and prepare for his long plane ride to North Carolina.

When Anthony departed to his next duty assignment, he had thirty days of vacation time before reporting to his next assignment. Anthony used the time to visit his family in North Carolina. During this time, he called Julie and gave her the news; their relationship was just friends. Anthony wanted to put away high school ties, he had in the past and think about the future. He thought about dedicating his self to his career, since he got promoted to a higher rank. Anthony had worked hard to receive the grade of Specialist; and he wanted to give a good impression to his next supervisor because he deserved it.

When Anthony arrived at his duty station in Ft Benning, Ga, he found out it was another Infantry base. Although, on the positive side, it did not matter because he was happy. Anthony was at home in America. If things got too bad, he was only six hours away from a visit to Winston Salem, NC. Anthony thought less about military women; now he was in the states. A non-military employee appeared to Anthony more suitable but; his intentions was not to find love at this stage. Anthony just wanted to get ahead financially in the military. Then, he figured love would come next, if it was meant to happen.

During the first weekend at his duty station, new soldiers as himself, influence him to go out to the popular hangouts. There was a new soldier named Simmons, who befriended Anthony. Simmons had the same military rank as Anthony and advised him to make friends with the local girls. One local girl introduced herself to Anthony at a popular club. Anthony thought; she was trying to be nice. Then, Simmons informed Anthony; the local girl named Rena was different.

Simmons replied, "Hey Anthony, I know you and I just met but; this girl is really interested in you. Her name is Rena; and she is dying to meet you".

Anthony replied, "Simmons are you tricking me".

Simmons replied, "I asked her out myself but; the girl told me no. She really likes you".

At first, Anthony figured; Simmons was playing a trick on him. Then, Anthony figured; for what. What reason do Simmons have to pull a trick like this? Rena eventually walked over to Anthony to introduce her friend Mary and herself. Mary was driving so, in her kindness, Rena and she invited Anthony with Simmons to breakfast. All of them had so much fun, they exchanged phone numbers between each other and made plans to meet the next day, where they were residing temporary. Anthony met up with Rena the next day, where she was residing temporary at her uncle's house.

Rena replied, "I am so happy to see you. Please, I would like you to meet my Aunt Bee and my Uncle A.B. Furthermore, I am visiting on spring break from college in my hometown in Macon, GA".

Anthony replied, "This is cool".

Anthony noticed a picture of Rena's Uncle A.B on the fireplace mantle. It highlighted his rank and duty assignment in the Army. The picture verified, Uncle A.B was the base personnel administration Commander Sergeant Major. Uncle A.B was Anthony's Post Commander and his Army supervisor. There was no other Army Sergeant on the entire base which hold a higher position than Uncle A.B. Anthony began to have anxiety. Here he was about to date Uncle A.B niece, his base supervisor. He politely notified Rena; her uncle was his supervisor.

Anthony notified Rena; he needed to return to the barracks. When he reached the barracks, he was not sure should he continue dating Rena. Anthony tried to think, what was the best solution. He informed his immediate supervisor in his work area.

Anthony replied, "Staff Sergeant Pipe, since you are my immediate supervisor, I would like to inform you; I am dating a girl, who is niece of the base Command Sergeant Major, do you have any advice on what I can do".

Staff Sergeant Pipe replied, "Specialist Anthony, you are talking about Command Sergeant Major A.B".

Anthony replied, "Yes".

Staff Sergeant Pipe replied, "I want you to call the girl right away. Whatever you do, don't get this girl upset. Command Sergeant Major A.B can make things difficult for everybody here. Specialist Anthony if you treat this girl right, with your time spent on this base, he will take care of you".

Anthony continues to follow Staff Sergeant Pipe advice and continue dating Rena. They started as friends but; it grew into a serious relationship quickly. Then, Rena got pregnant. Within a few months, they were engaged to be married.

Rena replied, "It is time for you to meet my entire family in Macon, Ga".

Anthony bought a car. Rena and he traveled to Macon, Ga to visit Rena's parents. The first step was to visit Rena's father. Rena's father was so happy; he had open arms at his door. He informed Anthony; it has been a short period which my daughter has been engaged to be married. I wonder; if you all, are old enough to decide to get married.

Anthony replied, "I know Rena and I are young but; we have grown to love each other".

Rena's father replied, "It is a good enough answer for me".

Then, Rena's cousin entered the room. This was the first time, Anthony met Rena's cousin named Linda.

Cousin Linda replied, "Anthony, it is nice to meet you. My cousin Rena and I are close as you will see in the future. I want you to promise me, you will do right by my cousin. My cousin may not always do right but; she means well".

Anthony replied, "I am not worried. If I know Rena, she is a good woman".

Then, Rena and Anthony met Rena's mother.

Rena's mother replied, "Anthony, I hope you know what you are doing, by getting married to my daughter. Rena is only twenty. How old is you?".

Anthony replied, "Nineteen".

Rena mother replied, "You are both so young. You have your entire lives in front of you. May god be with the both of you".

Rena's mother Madeline planned the entire wedding. She planned and arranged the wedding for six months later. Rena and Anthony were married soon after, with Rena's entire family attending. Then shortly, Rena had a baby girl. Within two years, Rena and Anthony were having their second child. Both children were girls. Anthony began to have financial problems with a wife and two children to care for. Rena was not working because she believed in staying home and taking care of the children. Anthony began pressuring her to get a job.

Rena replied, "If I want to work, I will get a job so; don't rush me".

Anthony replied, "The economy is bad so; you are going to have to get a job".

Rena called her cousin Linda. Cousin Linda visited Rena and Anthony. She stayed the entire weekend. Cousin Linda tried to console Rena and Anthony.

Cousin Linda replied, "Rena you know right from wrong; you have to help your husband if possible. Anthony is a good man; I see that with my own two eyes. He is taking care of you and your two beautiful children. You are blessed to have a wonderful husband in the military. Anthony, if you would, I would like to talk to you in private".

Anthony replied, "Sure Cousin Linda".

Linda replied, "I told you ahead of time; my cousin is not the best woman to marry. She means well anyways. I know, you are a good man. I thank you, for your patience with my cousin. I wish, you were my husband".

Cousin Linda kisses Anthony on the cheek and hold his hand.

Linda replied, "I wish, I had met you first. I would have made you my man. I have respect for my cousin. If you do not work out with my cousin, I want you to be mines".

Anthony replied, "Cousin Linda, I like you too but; I am married to Rena. I wouldn't even think about entertaining this idea".

Cousin Linda replied, "I knew, you would say this but; I just wanted you to know, how I feel"

Unfortunately, Rena died within five years of marriage. It was Anthony's worst day of his life. After the funeral, he notified his mom, he was leaving the military and relocating to North Carolina. Rena, she had died of a motor vehicle accident while trying to make it to a job interview. She had hired a cab driver to transport herself; and the driver had a head on collision. The last day, Anthony resided in Georgia with his children was one year after the funeral. Anthony new job was becoming a single father.

Anthony transferred out the regular Army to the Army Reserve in North Carolina at his hometown. His rank and title were now Staff Sergeant Anthony of the Personnel Military Command. Anthony retired out the military reserve and obtained employment eventually at the Winston Salem City Transportation. He worked part time for Greyhound Bus Lines. In the process of working at night his mother became the caretaker of his two kids during the day.

While Anthony entered his new acquired home in Winston Salem, NC, an unexpected phone call arrived. It was Cousin Linda from Georgia. Cousin Linda informed Anthony; she had heard he was doing well but he needs to come back to Georgia. She wants him to return to Atlanta, GA and take a break from his children.

Cousin Linda replied, "It has been a long time since we have socialized with each other; and it would do us good to visit each other in time of tragedy".

Anthony replied, "Maybe, I will take a visit".

In the city transportation building detailing buses, two gentlemen named Anthony and Kim are debating over Anthony's dilemma. Anthony wondered; should he take a trip to Atlanta or not.

Kim replied, "Why not! You know how, you want to see this fine cousin of yours named Linda".

Anthony replied, "I do have a crush on Cousin Linda; but this is my cousin"

Kim replied, "This is your cousin by marriage only. Besides, your wife passed away three years ago. Linda likes you; and it's time for you to move on with your life. How many times, do she have to invite you to her new house in Atlanta? You not scared are you".

Anthony replied, "No!".

Kim replied, "Well prove it and go".

The next day, Anthony confided to his mother about plans to go to Atlanta, GA.

Anthony replied, "Hi mom, I have some news, I want to share with you. I have been invited to see Cousin Linda in Atlanta, GA".

Dee Jackson replied, "Okay, but who is going to keep your children".

Anthony replied, "Mom, I was hoping you would watch the children, while I am gone".

Dee Jackson replied, "You know son, I have no problem keeping your children but; why do you want to see your cousin Linda for the weekend anyway? Cousin Linda supposed to be family, right".

Anthony replied, "Yes; but she is my wife's cousin. She really is not my cousin. Well technically, she is my cousin through marriage".

Dee Jackson replied, "I have no problem with it but; what are your children going to say".

Anthony replied, "I have not told the children".

Dee Jackson replied, "I like Linda. I think she is a nice girl. A matter of fact, I think she would be an upgrade compared to who you dated in the past. You informed, she is making a lot of money and have a big house. I just don't think it looks right in your children's eyes to be seeing your cousin in this fashion. You make sure, you tell your children; you plan to spend the weekend with Cousin Linda without them. Let me know in the process, how this goes".

Anthony replied, "Sure, I don't think, they would mind too much. They love Cousin Linda".

CHAPTER ELEVEN

# COUSIN LINDA

The next day, the children and Anthony are resting at their home in Winston Salem, NC. Anthony informs the children; he has some important news. He is going to Georgia; and he is going to spend the weekend with Cousin Linda.

Oldest daughter replied, "What for?"

Anthony replied, "I am taking a vacation from both my jobs to have fun".

Oldest daughter replied, "Can my sister and I go?"

Anthony replied, "No, not this time".

Oldest daughter replied, "Why?"

Anthony replied, "I want to be alone".

Oldest daughter replied, "You want to be alone on this trip with Cousin Linda".

Anthony replied, "Yes".

Oldest daughter replied, "You are going to be alone with Cousin Linda for the entire weekend?"

Anthony replied, "Yes".

Oldest daughter replied, "Do you like Cousin Linda?"

Anthony replied, "Yes, I think so".

Oldest daughter replied, "I thought Cousin Linda was your cousin".

Anthony replied, "She is my cousin by marriage only; but she is your cousin".

Oldest daughter replied, "I understand now; since mommy has gone, everybody on her side of the family is now fair game".

Anthony replied, "You are close but not everybody. Your mother has so many family members; how can I call everybody on her side family?"

Oldest daughter replied, "Well daddy, I think your children consents because if you marry Cousin Linda, we wouldn't have no problems.  We already consider her family anyways.

Anthony replied, "Good, I am glad you have no problems with this".

Anthony is on a Greyhound Bus to Atlanta, GA. He receives a phone call from his cousin Linda on his cell phone.

Cousin Linda replied, "Hey Anthony, I am glad you decided to come see me".

Anthony replied, "Sure, I thought about it being a long time, since I have seen you; and I do want to see, how well you are doing".

Cousin Linda replied, "I am doing good. What has it been, three years now? Last time, I have seen you, it was at my cousin funeral".

Anthony replied, "I know, it was a sad time".

Cousin Linda replied, "I have been thinking about you; and I keep feeling as if we need to spend some time together".

Anthony replied, "I feel the same way".

Cousin Linda replied, "I was going to pick you up at the bus station then, ran into a problem. Now, my friends will have to pick you up in my car for me".

Anthony replied, "Okay, it is fine".

In the bus station in Atlanta, GA, three women approached Anthony: a Puerto Rican named Halle, a Black woman named Eve, and a White woman named Becky. Anthony was beginning to feel agitated about someone picking him up from the bus station.

Anthony replied, “Where are these people. I thought, they would be here by now”.

The woman named Eve who arrived at the station replied, “Welcome to Atlanta Cousin Anthony. My name is Eve. This is Halle and last, this is Becky. We are here to take you home. Our needs are to make you feel at home and show you a good time while Linda is at work”.

Halle and Becky replied simultaneously, “Hello cousin”.

Eve replied, “Let us all be leaving the station because I do not want to be receiving another message from your Cousin Linda about picking you up. She Informed; you are her very important package”.

Anthony replied, “I agree with you on this note”.

After departing the bus terminal, Eve drove all four of them. She arrived at a driveway which led to a mansion sitting on an embankment above a thoroughfare. Across the street from the mansion was a dividing fenced wall which protected the neighbors from the highway traffic. The neighborhood across the street consisted of below income developments. The mansion upon sight, appeared to be newly remodel. While Anthony exited the vehicle and entered the residence, he is delighted with everything he observes so far.

Anthony replied, “This is a very nice place”.

Halle replied, “It should be, with all the money, which it drains from our income. Linda pays a lot of money to live here”.

Eve replied, “Just try to get settle in Anthony. I know, it was an uncomfortable trip on that bus. You rode from night until daylight. Make yourself at home, while I straighten up your bedroom. Then, I will show you, where your room is at”.

Anthony replied, “I sure appreciate this Eve”.

Becky replied, “When you finish, I am going to show you, where there is a nice place to eat in town”.

Anthony replied, “Thanks Becky”.

After Anthony settle down from unpacking, the three women returned from taking care of some business. Becky knocks on his bedroom door.

Becky replied, “May, I enter the room”.

Anthony replied, “Sure!”

Becky replied, “I was just wondering; are you ready for a little outing”.

Anthony replied, “Okay, where are we going?”

Becky replied, “The ladies and me are going to take you to a place and get you something to eat”.

Anthony replied, “This is good”.

The three women with Eve driving behind the steering wheel go up the main thoroughfare and transport Anthony to this neighborhood sports bar. In the sports bar, it has a slight crowd of people. The people are from all backgrounds with different languages and nationality. A large slightly overweight man with a big smile was standing behind the bar. He was speaking English and has a foreign ascent to his tone of voice.

Anthony replied, “Do this place have food?”

Eve replied, “I am not sure but; Becky loves this place”.

Becky replied, “Let me hold your hand and escort you to the bar owner. There is no need to worry about a thing. I have a credit line here. Just tell the owner, what you want. He will get it for you. We know each other well so; there is no problem with what you need”.

Anthony replied, “Thanks Becky because I am terribly hungry”.

Bar owner replied, “Hello sir, my name is Al. Big Al is what they call me. If you need anything, I am the owner, bartender, and server. I hear, you are a friend to the women and my good friend Becky. Any friend of Becky's is a friend of mines. What can I do for you?"

Becky replied, "Thanks, Big Al. Furthermore Anthony, the other women and I must run off again for a second. I have no fear because Big Al is going to take care of you. We will be right back".

Anthony replied, "You women are the busiest people, even for the city of Atlanta".

Big Al replied, "Alright big fella, let me see what you would like to have".

Anthony replied, "Whatever is the house special will be fine. Just put it on Becky's credit".

Four hours have pass; and it is becoming later in the afternoon. Anthony is finished with his meal and drank three beers. There was no sign of the women; and he begins to feel abandon. He noticed people in the bar having a good time. A gay couple was consisting of men enjoying themselves. Then, group parties entered and left the club; but all had a good time. He wonders; where are the women. Big Al returned behind the bar and bended over to ask him a question.

Big Al replied, "Heard anything from the women?"

Anthony replied, "Not recently. It is getting late in the afternoon now. I am ready to leave now".

Big Al replied, "You know, I can call Becky, if you want me to".

Anthony replied, "Would you please".

Big Al replied, "How do you know Becky?"

Anthony replied, "Becky lives with my cousin in a big house down the main road".

Big Al replied, "Which one is your cousin?"

Anthony replied, "Neither one of these three women. She is at work".

Big Al replied, "What other woman; there is only three women who lives in the big house down the road. Becky, Eve and Halle are the only women, I know who lives in the big house".

Anthony replied, "My cousin Linda lives there. She owns the house".

Big Al replied, "I do not know a Linda. Maybe, every now and then; I do see other women visit once and awhile".

Anthony replied, "A nice looking woman, maybe 5 foot 5 with long black hair".

Big Al replied, "Yes".

Anthony replied, "This is Linda. She owns the place".

A nice-looking Toyota arrives at Big Al sports bar. It parks in the parking lot with three attractive women. Eve is driving, Becky was on the passenger side and Halle was sitting in the back about to make a grand entrance. Becky decided to exit the vehicle and notify Anthony; they have arrived. When Becky entered through the front door, she observed Anthony appearing to be very unhappy, sitting at the bar.

Becky replied, "Hey Anthony, how is my Carolina visitor doing?"

Anthony replied, "Don't hey me, I have been waiting on you for the longest. I was ready to go, about two hours ago".

Becky replied, "I know! We took a long time making it back to you. We had a lot of business to take care of. I should have told you; we are college students at the university up the road. It was crowded in the enrollment office. Halle, she is so slow".

Anthony replied, "Well, I am ready to go. I am tired; and I want to take a bath".

Becky replied, "The women was coming in to mingle with you".

Anthony replied, "I am going to the car".

Becky replied, "I am coming behind you".

Becky and Anthony returned to the vehicle. Eve and Halle are getting out the vehicle.

Anthony replied, "Women are we ready to go".

Halle replied, "Leave for what, I am ready to get my boogie on".

Eve replied, "I was just going to come in and ask you Anthony, did you want to dance".

Anthony replied, "No, I am ready to go. I want to talk to Linda".

Halle replied, "I talk to Linda. I told her everything was fine. She has become ill at work. She left me a message to tell you; it will be a little longer before she comes home. The medicine she took at work, has made her sick; and she has decided to stay overnight, until she feels better".

Anthony replied, "Is this bad luck or what?"

Eve replied, "Okay Anthony, do not talk negative. I am going to take you home. We just have one stop; and it is to the gas station to buy some whatnots".

Anthony replied, "All right".

All four people sitting in the vehicle depart the sports bar. They arrived shortly at the nifty store: a local gas station which serves utility items across the street from a poor neighborhood. All the women exited the vehicle and enters the gas station. Anthony steps out the vehicle to stretch his legs. He noticed a rocking chair beside the station and an older man sitting on a dirt embankment behind the chair. Anthony decided to sit in the chair to think. Then about the same time, a different older man walks across the street coming out of the poor neighborhood and speaks to him.

The older neighborhood man replied, "Hey young fella, you're not from around here; now, are you?"

Anthony replied, "No, but what about it?"

The neighborhood man replied, "I want you to read something".

Anthony replied, "Look sir, I really am not trying to read anything. I am just sitting here waiting on my friends. I am too tired and sleepy".

The neighbor man replied, "Okay, but this is important information to our neighborhood".

Anthony replied, "Okay, I will look at it. Now, I am finish; so, can you leave me alone now?"

Older background man behind the chair replied, "Hey old man, I know you. There you go always messing with customers; why you bothering folks? He is not bothering you".

The neighborhood man replied, "I am not causing any harm".

The women exiting the store replied, "Old man go back to your neighborhood. Nobody wants to be harassed. This man is from North Carolina visiting. Please leave him alone".

Eve replied, "Anthony, let's everybody leave".

Anthony replied, "Thanks, girls".

The women and Anthony arrived from the nifty store at the mansion. After Eve parked the vehicle in the driveway, she turned the engine off and invited everyone inside for a homemade dinner. Anthony informed the women; he is going to take a bath. Halle informed everyone; she is going to run bathwater for her middle-aged school daughter. Becky was in the process of putting her waterbed up and had to fill water in her mattress. While Eve had to wash dishes, before she could start cooking dinner.

Anthony replied, "This has been a long day. I am going to call Linda. Hey Linda, how are you feeling".

Linda replied, "Hey Anthony, I am sorry about getting sick. I hope the women have been treating you nice".

Anthony replied, "Well, I guess they are doing their best".

Linda replied, "I hope so because I have something to tell you. I am going to be honest. I work for the government as a test patient".

Anthony replied, "Okay!"

Linda replied, "They gave me some medicine. It made me sick. If possible, can you stay the entire week? I am sure, I will be home shortly".

Anthony replied, "Sure, I will try".

Linda replied, "Wonderful because we really need to see each other".

Anthony replied, "Okay Linda, I am going to take me a bath and relax in your glorious bathroom".

Halle receives a phone call from her daughter's school; her daughter's school bus was in an accident. She notified the other woman; and they rushed to the car to find the bus. They observed the accident was right up the street. The women then decided to walk to the accident and not take the automobile. While this was occurring, Anthony was finishing his bath; and he had no knowledge of the accident.

Anthony decided to check on the women. He heard water running, while walking down the hallway in the mansion. Then, he witnesses water running out of the bathtub in the bathroom where Halle was to give her daughter a bath. He shouts for the women but no answer. Then, Anthony entered Becky's bedroom and her waterbed mattress had a leak. Water was pouring out her waterbed mattress. Anthony shouts the women names but still no response. Last, he decided to walk through the kitchen and noticed, dishwater was overflowing from the kitchen sink.

Tension begins to rise inside him. He thinks to himself, why these women just abandon the place. These women are not fit to stay anywhere. I have come down to the last straw. I am going to fix the water from running everywhere, pack my bags and go back to North Carolina. I want to have a reunion with Linda but; it is not worth dealing with a whole lot of mess. After he packs, he waves goodbye to his room and carries his bag out the front door.

The women approach the accident scene. They see the school bus driver, as she was answering questions from a police officer. The women begin to approach the bus driver, as the bus driver and police officer paused. Then, the bus begin observing the women walking towards their direction.

Halle replied, "Good even everyone. Anybody have seen a little Spanish girl about this high".

Bus driver replied, "Yes mam. She is over there with the rest of the students in a group".

Halle replied, "Thank God! Thank you so much bus driver for keeping my daughter and everyone safe".

Bus driver replied, "No problem; but to be cautious, you might want to check her for bruises. I slammed on the breaks pretty hard to prevent from hitting anything".

Becky replied, "Can anybody tell me what happen here?"

Police officer replied, "Yes, it was some old man and a couple of kids out in the neighborhood across the street. They were throwing rocks with a note attached at the bus, while the bus was traveling down the road".

Eve replied to the Police Officer, "I think, I know the old man who you are referring about. Will you allow me to call a guest of the family because I believe he can be a witness to something.

Police officer replied, "Sure thing".

Eve calls Anthony on the phone. Anthony answers his cell phone.

Anthony replied on the phone, "Hello, who this".

Eve replied, "Hey Anthony, what are you doing".

Anthony replied, "I am leaving. Right now, I am walking to the bus station".

Eve replied, "Why, what is wrong?"

Anthony replied, "I can't take it anymore. This whole trip has become a waste of time".

Eve replied, "A waste of time for who?"

Anthony replied, "A waste of time for me because I have not seen Linda. Second, her roommates do not know anything about hospitality. Last, after I finished my bath, I find water flooding in three rooms of the house".

Eve replied, "Look Anthony, I am sorry you feel this way. As soon I get through talking to you, I am going to call Linda; and tell her she needs to talk to you. Right now, Anthony we have an emergency. I need you to tell me, when we were at the gas station, did you read a note this old man was showing you".

Anthony replied, "Yes, I read it. It stated, 'Destroy the local businesses, the schools and neighborhoods because this area do not support black elderly people".

Eve replied, "Oh my goodness! Anthony can you just stick around for a while; so, you can be a witness to the police, what this old man is trying to do".

Anthony replied, "Why, what's up?

Eve replied, "This old man from the neighborhood across the street has gone overboard. He has thrown rocks at Halle's daughter's school bus and cause an accident. We women are here at the scene right now".

Anthony replied, "Look Eve; I am here already at the bus station and have figured it out, what time the bus should be arriving. What I will do is give the police officer in the station a signed letter in writing, which an old man in the area has issued a threat on the local neighborhood".

Eve replied, "Thank you, Anthony".

Anthony replied, "Oh no; Eve, I have to go".

Eve replied, "What is the matter? Is that your bus?"

Anthony replied, "No, it is that old man from the neighborhood across the street; and he has kids with him. He is waiting in the passenger drop off area".

Anthony hangs his cell phone up with Eve and attempts to notify the police officer in the bus terminal. He alerts the police officer of an old man with kids carrying a large backpack and possibly a suspect to an accident. The police officer informed him; it was okay if the old man wanted to wait in the passenger drop off area for a passenger because the old man wasn't disturbing anyone. Then, he told Anthony to remain quiet, while he waited for his bus and allow the police to do their job.

Shortly afterwards, the Greyhound bus showing Charlotte at the top approached. The old man announced to the kids; everybody gets ready. When the kids heard this, they began digging for rocks out the old man backpack. Anthony walked up quietly behind the old man and apprehended the man. Other passengers who were departing apprehend the kids. The police officer running behind arrested the violators.

Police officer replied, "Thank you folks for your help".

Bus driver replied, "The citizen over there saved the day. What is your name so?"

Anthony replied, "Anthony, sir. It is nothing".

Police officer replied, "Anthony, okay! I am going to write your name down in my report".

Anthony replied, "Hey officer, before you place him in jail, can I have a word with the suspect".

Police officer replied, "Sure, just don't take too long".

Anthony replied to the old man, "Why old man; what reasons do you want to destroy your own neighborhood?"

Neighborhood old man replied, "Young fella, I can't explain nothing to you because you probably never lost anything you love. I grew up in this area. These people use to respect the elderly people. It was a prosperous black community until those foreigners started moving into our area. Now the prices are jacked up and soon, they are going to start tearing our low-income homes down. Then, what am I going to do".

Anthony replied, "I do understand. What you loved in the community is gone. What you must do is move on and adjust to the changes. You cannot bring the past back through violence. The only way to cope with life is to adjust to something new and appreciate it".

Anthony thinks about his life; wife deceased and how he must adjust to life. He thinks about Linda, how he needs to pursue a new love and the time he had being single. Afterwards, he called Eve to apologize for the harsh statements and requested her to pick him up from the bus station. He knows, it would be impolite not to stick around and to see Linda. Anthony receives a call from Linda.

Linda replied, "Hello Anthony".

Anthony replied, "Linda, can I explain why, I left the house".

Linda replied, "Sure, you can".

Anthony replied, "When I decided to visit you, I took a leap of faith. It took my co-worker to convince me to move on with my life. I really miss my wife of five years. Then, meeting your roommates made me review myself. I realized there is a need for patience; and I cannot give up so easy. The suspect also taught me to let the past go and move on. In conclusion, I do not want to become as the old man in the neighborhood. I want to be in love again with someone and enjoy life again. If possible, I would like to consider taking you out on dates".

Linda replied, "Oh Anthony! I feel the same way; but I figure it was too sudden".

Anthony replied, "I know, it is sudden; but let's give it a try".

Linda replied, "Yes, I would enjoy this. I am feeling fine now. Tell the women to come pick me up. We can go on a date tomorrow".

## The End